D1408392

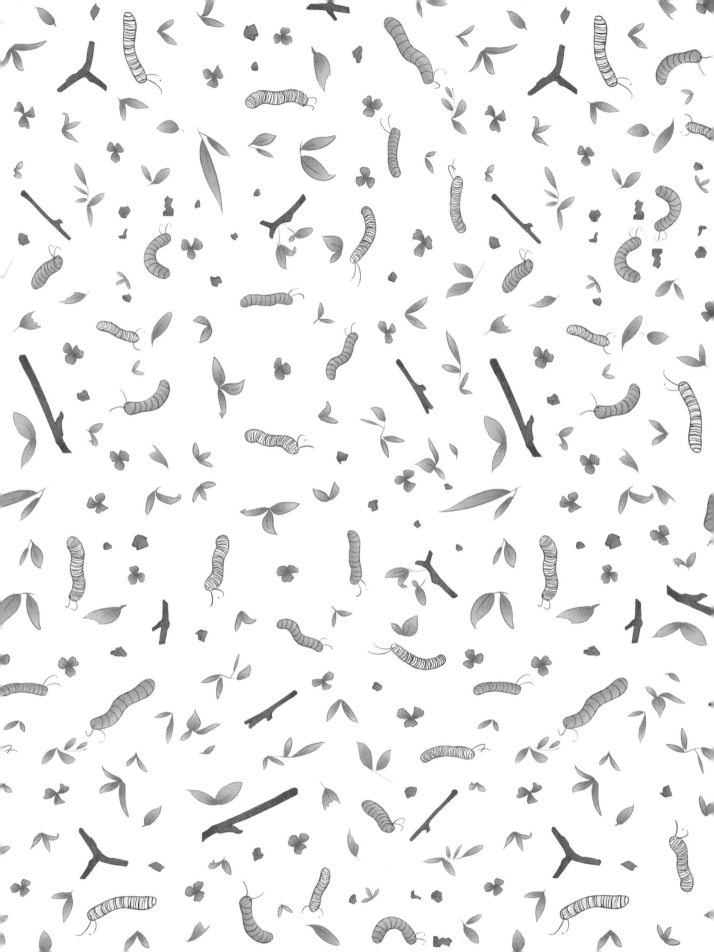

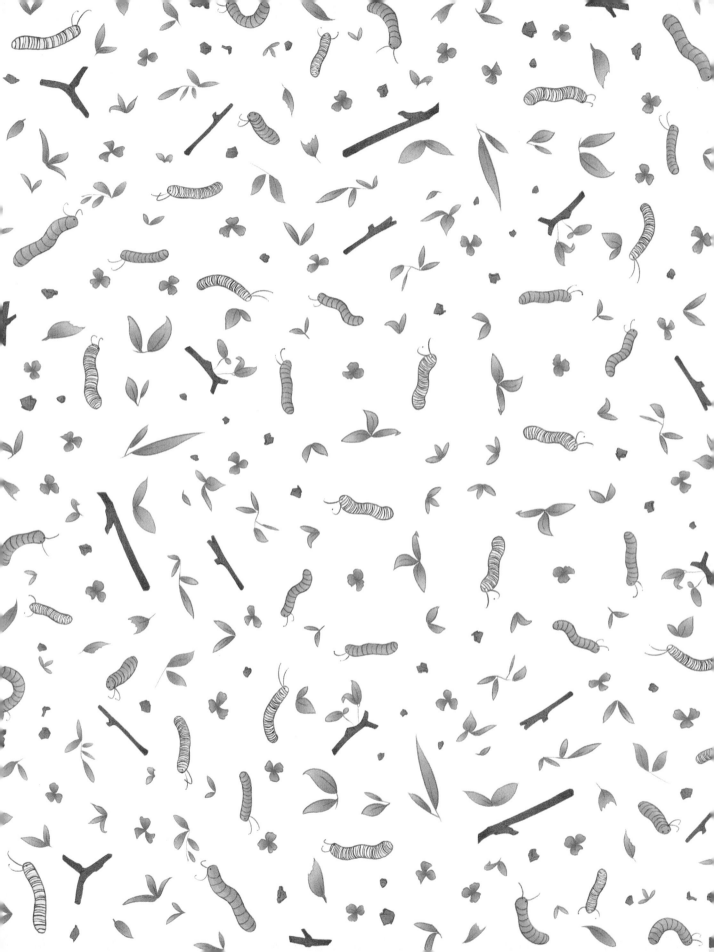

CATERPILLARLAND

by Roxanne Beck

Illustrated by Jessica Flores

To Josephine—
Fly!!
Love,
Roxanne

Chakra 4 Publishing

Printed in the United States of America
First Edition, 2015
ISBN 978-0-692-45349-0

Chakra 4 Publishing
15206 Dickens St., #7
Sherman Oaks, CA 91403

For Grace and James

And for my mother

ACKNOWLEDGMENTS

I would like to thank my wonderful family for their unwavering love and loyalty. Much gratitude also goes to my brilliant editors: Cynthia Alcott, Bonnie Barnes, and Betty Ulrey. Readers who have been extremely generous with their encouragement and support for *Caterpillarland* include Lea Black, Cynthia Chapman, Cathey Coulter, Stephanie Fain, Mark Harris, Lacy James, Sea Parsons, and Russelle Marcato Westbrook. Last but not least, I'd like to thank Jessica Flores for her beautiful illustrations.

Chapter One

It was a beautiful, breezy spring day. The whole countryside was absolutely bursting with flowers—primroses, bluebonnets, daisies, jasmine, azaleas, poppies, daffodils, camellias, magnolias, coneflowers, daffodils, even Black-eyed Susans. Not a single human could be seen within a square country mile, which was just fine with the squirrels, rabbits, and deer. Robins, purple martins, blackbirds and sparrows sang out boldly, looking for mates.

As the sun was beginning to set, a cloud of what looked like orange dust began to materialize in the northeastern sky. Gradually it got larger and larger, until it became obvious that it wasn't a dust cloud.

There were dozens . . .

No, hundreds . . .

No, *thousands*, of monarch butterflies! They were on their way from Maine to Mexico for the winter. Even though this particular bunch had never been there before, somehow they knew the way. Leading them was Marcus, a dignified male. He scanned the earth below looking for a place to rest for the night. "Okay, guys, this is it," he called out. "Make sure you have a buddy, and watch out for humans!"

"Woohoo!" cried the younger butterflies as they zoomed in for a landing. Soon they were all on the ground, forming an enormous orange-and-black quilt. Each one picked a flower or a tree blossom and drank deep of the nectar.

"Wow, was I thirsty!" said one.

"Me too!" said another. "Whatcha got over there?"

"Phlox. Good stuff," said the first.

For a few minutes everybody was silent as they drank their fill. Then, unable to contain herself any longer, a young female voice piped up.

"Ahhh! Now *that* is special."

The voice was attached to a rare orange-and-*blue* butterfly, who stuck out from the flock like a tiny, neon sign. Her name was Monique, and she was Marcus' daughter. (Her mother was also an orange-and-blue butterfly, but she had died when Monique was still a caterpillar.) She liked being different, and although she was the envy of all the other girl butterflies, Monique didn't think much about her looks. Notwithstanding her youth, she was a nectar *connoisseur* and could already detect "notes" of pear in pansies. Again she sank her *proboscis* into the middle of the yellow coneflower and sipped. Mickey, a young monarch who had been admiring Monique from a distance, zipped over.

"Hey, Monique! Need a buddy?"

"Oh, I'm good, thanks," she replied, barely glancing at him as she switched to a cluster of daffodils. Another boy, Marty, flew over and hovered above Monique. He cleared his throat loudly, as if he was about to say something very important.

"Excuse me, Ms. Monique! I've been meaning to tell you—I think you've got the prettiest wings in the whole flock! Wanna be my buddy?"

"Hey! I already asked her," Mickey interrupted.

"Why don't you let the lady speak for herself?" said Marty.

"Okay, I will," Mickey retorted. "Tell him, Monique!"

Monique, who was used to this kind of attention, coughed politely. "You're both very nice, but I already have a buddy," she said. "Now, if you'll excuse me, I have to get back to my tasting.

"Okay, maybe next time," said Mickey, flying off.

"Enjoy, beautiful," said Marty.

Nearby, a couple of female butterflies looked up from their dinner and sniffed. "Hm! She's not that pretty. I mean, what's so special about *blue*?"

Overhearing this, Monique blushed and flew over to a patch of peonies. She sipped for a while, then looked around. Suddenly she noticed something that made her gasp. It was a pink "Knockout" rose bush, sitting improbably between a big oak tree and a small creek bed.

"Oh, my gosh!" she said. "Knockouts!" She started to take off, but a pair of yellow-and-black wings wrapped around her from behind and covered her eyes.

"Excuse me, miss!" said a familiar voice, trying to sound tough. "Where's your buddy?"

"Tiger!" said Monique in an exasperated voice. "If you sneak up on me like that one more time, I'll—I'll—"

"What? Kiss me?"

Tiger, a yellow swallowtail butterfly, was Monique's childhood friend. They had burst out of their cocoons within seconds of each other. He had gotten separated from his family a few days later, and Monique's dad had allowed him to fly with the monarchs. Tiger was very near-sighted and wore large, black, horn-rimmed glasses.

"You know I don't think of you that way, Tiger," said Monique.

"Aw, come on, lighten up!" he teased her. "I was just kidding."

"Fine," Monique said impatiently as she flew to the rose bush. "I just want to taste as many flowers as I can before we have to leave, and there are so many to choose from. I'm running out of time!"

"Okay, okay! Stick with ordinary old roses if you want. I just saw a big butterfly bush over that way, but it's outside the designated area, so I guess you wouldn't be interested," said Tiger mischievously.

"Butterfly bush! Where? Where?"

Now, Tiger knew that the mere mention of the words "butterfly bush" would stop Monique dead in her tracks. It's a well-known fact that butterfly bushes produce some of the most delicious nectar in the world, but Monique had never tasted it.

Tiger flew off, yelling back at her. "Come with me, I'll show you!"

"Wait! *Where* is it?" panted Monique, trying to catch up.

"Over here! You're going to flip out when you taste it!" They flew until they reached a line of trees at the edge of the open field. If they had looked behind them, they would have noticed that they could no longer see any of the other butterflies. They hesitated for a moment, then flew deeper into the forest. And finally, there it was, right in front of them: a huge bush covered with cone-shaped purple blossoms. "*Voila*, babe!" Tiger announced.

"Wow!" cried Monique. Beating him to it, she somewhat rudely took the first drink. "Mmmm! Amazing!"

"Hey, don't I at least get a thank you?" asked Tiger.

"Of course. Thank you, I owe you one." She flew over to Tiger and kissed him on the cheek, knocking his glasses sideways. Tiger grinned proudly. "Looks like there's plenty for both of us," said Monique.

"Nah, I had plenty before," said Tiger. "I'd better get back—it'll be worse if your dad finds out we're both missing. If you're not back by sundown, I'm coming after you. Okay?"

"Okay," Monique agreed. But she was already busy sipping nectar and didn't even notice Tiger fly away.

For the next few minutes Monique drank and drank. She was so happy that she even closed her eyes, which is something that all monarchs have been taught never to do, unless they're sleeping, of course. She had no clue that two human butterfly catchers were spying on her from just a few yards away.

"Look at *that*!" whispered a Short Man excitedly as he peeked around a tree. "An orange-and-blue one!"

"I see it, I see it," said his companion, a Tall Man. "And it's gonna look great on my wall!"

"Are you kidding? I saw it first!" snapped the Short Man, pointing his net at the Tall Man like a sword.

"Tell it to the judge," said the Tall Man, making a run for the bush. He raised his net and was about to bring it down on Monique when the Short Man gave him a sharp kick in the knee, knocking him to the ground.

"Ow!" cried the Tall Man. "So you want to get nasty about it!"

"Sorry! It was an accident," the Short Man lied. By now Monique had heard the commotion and darted away.

"Come 'ere, you!" said the Short Man.

Now to be honest, Monique was feeling a little sluggish from all that nectar. She had never seen a human butterfly hunter but had always thought that she could easily out-fly them. She hid inside the butterfly bush as the Short Man swatted at her, jumping up and down with excitement. Back on his feet, the Tall Man spotted her colorful wings amongst the leaves.

"I've got it!"

"No, I've got it!" said the Short Man. *Whoosh!* went the nets.

"Hm! I'm a she, not an 'it'—isn't it obvious?" Monique muttered, flying up into a tree as the butterfly catchers swatted their nets in vain. But they weren't giving up so easily. They guarded the butterfly bush as if it were a pot of gold, craning their necks every which way for another glimpse of the rare butterfly. Watching them, she pouted. She would have to give up the butterfly bush and return to the flock.

But which way was that? Monique looked to the west, where the sun was sinking below the horizon. "Tiger!" she yelled. But there was no answer.

Monique decided to fly north, since she couldn't remember flying into the sun on the way to the butterfly bush, and she was pretty sure they hadn't flown east. The sun was setting fast now, and she was having a hard time seeing more than a few feet in front of her. She had drunk so much nectar that her body was almost twice as big as it had been only an hour before. After a few minutes, it seemed that she'd only flown a few feet! Stopping to rest on a large rock, she heard the unmistakable sound of human footsteps. Looking over her shoulder, she saw the Short Man and the Tall Man running towards her. She lifted off and tried to gain altitude, flapping her wings frantically. *Whoosh!*

Monique desperately looked around for a place to hide. The forest was thick with trees, but most of them were so tall that she couldn't reach their branches. *WHOOSH!* A net grazed her wing, knocking her off course. Below her, she spotted some gnarly tree roots and dived for them, hoping to camouflage herself. At the same moment the Tall Man was caught by a low-hanging branch and fell backwards with a crash.

"Have a nice trip!" the Short Man snorted. He brought his net down on the roots with a *smack* and carefully took a jar out of his knapsack. He lifted the net, but there was no butterfly.

"Where'd it go?" he yelled.

"Owwwww!" groaned the Tall Man, still flat on his back. "Serves you right if it got away!"

Monique seemed to have disappeared into thin air. If not for one bit of very good luck, she would have been doomed. As the Short Man's net came down on top of her, she had noticed a tiny crevice in the ground between the roots. She had jumped into it and flattened her wings, holding herself up by rigidly extending her antennae against each side of the narrow cranny.

She waited in this position until she could no longer hear the humans' frustrated mumblings. "Maybe they've given up," she thought. But when she tried to lift herself out of the crack, her wings wouldn't flap. The crevice was too tight, and she began to slip.

"Whoa!" she said, bracing herself. But the ground was slick and slimy, and she couldn't hang on. She slid farther down into the crevice, which was getting wider. "Help!" she cried out. "*Heeellllp!*"

Gravity was now sucking her down into the wet earth. The crevice opened up more as she fell, but it was too late to stop her momentum. She fell and fell and fell, almost as if she was being sucked down into the earth. Finally, she landed hard on a cold and slippery surface.

"Owww," she moaned softly in the pitch-blackness, which was darker than any moonless night. "Where am I?"

Monique had never been underground before. She didn't even know there *was* such a thing as "underground." She had simply been flying and floating and drinking nectar for as long as she could remember. You might say she was a bit of a princess, but with no fairy godmother in sight.

"HELLO! Is anybody there?" Her voice echoed back to her from the far corners of the cave: *"ANYBODY THERE? ANYBODY THERE? ANYBODY THERE?"* As her eyes adjusted, she began to make out the forms of big, icy things that looked like giant carrots hanging from the ceiling and jutting up from the ground. If Monique had known anything about caves, she would have known that the icy things were stalactites (the ones hanging down from the roof of the cave) and stalagmites (the ones sticking up from the ground). All she knew was that she was in a very unpleasant, cold, gray place that had no sky, no sunshine and, more importantly, *no flowers*.

"Hey! Can somebody help me? I—I have to get out of here!"

Again, Monique's voice echoed back: *"OUT OF HERE! OUT OF HERE!"* When she turned around she saw not one, but *hundreds*, of cracks in the cave's roof, and it was impossible to tell which one she had fallen through. She was trapped.

Chapter Two

Realizing the seriousness of her situation, Monique swallowed hard. "Stay calm," she told herself. "That's what Tiger would say. In a crisis, you have to stay calm." She tried humming for a few seconds, but it didn't work. Not knowing the way out of the cave, she was a little afraid to leave the ledge she was perched on. Then she heard a weird noise in the distance that sounded like hundreds of tiny little drums, or—*feet*. She squinted, and saw what was making the noise: hundreds of worm-like creatures, marching in formation. It sounded like they were singing. She flew off the ledge and landed on a smooth stalagmite, trying to get a better look.

"Work, work, work, work, work until you die. Spin that silk, and don't ask why! Worms do as they're told, they don't whine, they don't cry. Just work, work, work, work, work, work until you die!"

Monique's eyes nearly popped out of her head. Those weren't bugs or worms, but *caterpillars*—hundreds of them, marching like common army ants! Not just yellow-and-black monarch caterpillars, but caterpillars of all shapes, sizes and colors. They looked tired, and some of them even looked *old*. "Old caterpillars? That's impossible," she shuddered. "I've gotta get out of here!" In the distance, a few shafts of dull moonlight fell from tiny cracks in the cave's ceiling, half-heartedly illuminating a factory-like building with the insignia of a Death's-head moth above the door. Suddenly the door swung open and dozens of caterpillars emerged. The new group of caterpillars then marched in, single file. It was shift-switching time.

Monique shut her eyes and shook her head, as if trying to erase the memory of what she'd just seen. She was already thirsty and in need of a drink, so she flew further into the cave. Soon she came to a small building with a flat roof that appeared to have been made out of mud. Over the door was a sign that read "*Wormland Academy*." (That was of no help to Monique, who had never been to school and couldn't read a word.) She flew to the building's one window and looked inside. A classroom full of young caterpillars—some striped, some in solid colors—sat at their desks, writing in their notebooks just like human children do. They looked like they'd been writing for a very long time, and no one was smiling.

At the front of the classroom, a giant snail barked instructions. "Keep going, students! It is very important to remember who and what we are, is it not? Tomorrow we shall resume our silk-spinning lessons."

On the blackboard the words "*A worm is a worm is a worm*" were written in perfect letters. Monique gasped in horror. The teacher, whose name was Mrs. Beige, waddled over to her desk and picked up a book entitled *The Importance of Being Average*. As she read, a smug smile crept across her face.

At the back of the classroom, a bright-green caterpillar let out a big sigh and stopped writing. He looked up to make sure Mrs. Beige wasn't looking at him, and quietly turned to a clean sheet of paper in his notebook. Glancing at Claire, the pretty girl caterpillar sitting next to him, he quickly began sketching her.

"You're going to get in trouble, Charley," she whispered.

"Not if I finish before she catches me," Charley whispered back, his pencil flying over the page.

By now Charley had given Claire's likeness a shy, Mona-Lisa smile (even though Charley had never seen the "Mona Lisa"). Lewis Beasley, the caterpillar sitting in front of Charley, turned around to see what was going on. Lewis was the sort of kid who got a big kick out of ratting on other students. He raised his hand. "Excuse me, Mrs. Beige? Littlefield's drawing one of those 'pictures' again."

"Tattletale!" whispered Claire.

"Charley!" Mrs. Beige bellowed. "Is that true?"

"But we already *know* we're worms," said Charley. "It's boring!"

Mrs. Beige's eyes narrowed dangerously. "Come here! And bring that paper with you," she said.

Charley tore the drawing out of his notebook and slowly approached the teacher's desk. He handed it to the snail, who immediately wadded it up and threw it in the trashcan without even glancing at it.

"As you well know, deviance of any kind at Wormland Academy is strictly prohibited," intoned Mrs. Beige. "In the future you will do the repetition as instructed. Is that clear?"

"Yes, ma'am. But—"

"There are no *buts*! Back to your seat," she hissed. "You will stay after school and write the exercise an additional one thousand times!"

Charley blushed a deep red, bowed his head and fidgeted, but none of his feet moved.

"I SAID, BACK TO YOUR SEAT!" yelled Mrs. Beige dramatically, her eyes nearly bulging out of their sockets. After a full three seconds, Charley finally spoke up.

"I'm not going to do it anymore," he said simply.

The class gasped in unison; Mrs. Beige's jaw dropped. Then Charley began to quiver, and looked like he might throw up. His skin began to peel right off of him, revealing an even brighter shade of green, as bright as the grass on a summer lawn. Charley kicked his old skin away from himself, his cheeks burning with embarrassment.

This was the first time anything like this had happened in Mrs. Beige's classroom. "Children, do not panic," said Mrs. Beige evenly. "Stay in your seats. *You!* Come with me," she commanded Charley, her teeth clenched.

Monique, who had witnessed the whole scene from outside the window, was in a state of shock. What kind of a place was this, where caterpillars were reprimanded for something as normal as shedding their skins? She didn't want to watch anymore, so she flew up to the roof of the school, flattened her wings and closed her eyes. Maybe if she could just sleep for a while, she would wake up to find that she was back with Tiger and the rest of her flock, and this had all been a very bad dream.

In the classroom, the students chattered nervously about Charley's act of rebellion. "My mom said that when that happens, it means you've got 'changing fever'!" said one.

"And there isn't any cure for it," said another.

"Yeah, that's what mine said, too," said a third.

"Changing fever?" said the first. "But isn't that—"

"CONTAGIOUS!!!" cried all the caterpillars. And they all stampeded out of the room and down the hallway, knocking Mrs. Beige and Charley over in the process. The school doors flew open and Mrs. Beige came rolling out like a runaway tire in the midst of the screaming mob. Only Charley and Claire were left in the classroom.

"You'd better get home," said Claire.

"Right. If anything happens to me, I just want to tell you that—"

"Don't say it!" said Claire. "Just go!"

Charley, his new green skin glowing like a traffic light, impulsively gave Claire a kiss on the cheek, causing her face turned almost as red as Charley's had been moments earlier. Then he grabbed one of her hands and they ran out of the school, heading toward the rows of identical mud huts that served as the caterpillars' homes.

Meanwhile, Mrs. Beige's shell was rolling out of control, toward a clump of stalagmites. "Guards! Guards! Emergency! Emergency!" she screamed from inside it. A number of large, brown cockroaches wearing uniforms emerged from out of nowhere; some chased the students, while others followed Mrs. Beige. Finally she crashed into the rocks, spun up into the air for a few seconds, and landed with a *splat* on the ground right in front of the confused guards. She poked her head out of her shell.

"Changing fever! Changing fever! Notify the queen immediately," she gasped, and fainted.

The guards turned and goose-stepped off toward a large, wooden structure that looked like a giant birdcage. It hung suspended from the roof of the cave and was covered in tatters of brightly colored material that ruffled toward the ground.

Monique surveyed the situation from the roof of the school building. She could see the cockroaches marching toward the birdcage, while most of the caterpillars had made it to their homes by now. Catching a glimpse of Charley's glowing green skin in the distance, she followed him.

Charley threw open the door of his house and rushed in, locking the door behind him. A pudgy, older caterpillar sat in his lounge chair watching a ballgame on a very old, black-and-white TV.

"Where's Mom?" panted Charley.

Oooh! So close!" said Charley's dad to the TV, ignoring his son.

Charley ran into the kitchen. A female caterpillar wearing an apron stood at the stove preparing a meager supper of "stick casserole."

"Hey, Mom," said Charley, trying to sound casual. "Where's my anti-change medication?"

"In the bathroom, where it usually is," she said, without turning around. Charley dashed into the bathroom and slammed the door. He heard his mom call out, "Why are you home early?"

"No reason!" Charley answered.

"Are you sick?"

"Nope! Everything's fine," he answered airily.

But Cathy knew better. She frowned and went into the living room.

"Fred! Did you see Charley when he came in?"

"Uh . . . yeah," said Fred, his eyes glued to the TV set.

"How did he look to you?" she asked.

"Fine. He looked fine."

"Well, he's acting weird," she whispered, and sat down in the lounge chair next to her husband.

"Aw, come on, you stupid cockroach ref! Get some new glasses!" Fred yelled. Cathy sighed and picked up the newspaper, *The Wormland Daily Update*.

In the bathroom, Charley was staring at himself in the mirror. His cheeks were still crimson red, his skin a dazzling, emerald green. He took a pill bottle out of the medicine chest. It read:

"Anti-Change Medication. Take two per day; do not miss a dose."

Charley opened it, tossed all of its contents into his mouth, and swallowed. Taking a deep breath, he relaxed slightly. Then he took some talcum powder out of the cabinet and patted it on his face in an effort to tone down his cheeks. The result was disappointing. "Freak," said Charley. He washed his face and opened the bathroom door a crack, making sure the coast was clear. Then he darted into his bedroom.

On an easel in Charley's room was a large sketchpad, with the beginnings of a self-portrait. In the picture, Charley stood beside a flying machine, beaming like a proud pilot. In fact, pictures of wings were tacked up all over Charley's bedroom walls. "Who am I kidding?" he said, tearing the picture off the easel. "Only the queen and her son can fly!" He said the last sentence as if he were mimicking someone. He wadded it up and threw it in the corner, then started yanking all the other pictures off the walls. Finally he collapsed on his bed and cried into a pillow, hoping no one could hear.

In the living room, Fred's ballgame was suddenly interrupted by loud, official-sounding music.

"Oh, brother—not again!" said Fred.

"And now, for a message from Queen Martha," said the announcer. On the screen appeared a very unattractive Death's-head moth, who looked as if she must be at least seventy-five years old. She wore an elaborate silk get-up and a tiara on top of her furry head.

"Good evening, citizens of Wormland," she said, and smiled ghoulishly. "With grave displeasure, we must report there was an outbreak of changing fever at Wormland Junior High today. The cause is simple: The guilty worm was not taking his anti-change medication as instructed." When she said "guilty worm," a photo of Charley flashed on the screen!

"Charley?" exclaimed Cathy, two of her "hands" flying to her mouth.

"What the—" said Fred.

"Therefore," the moth-queen continued, "by royal command, all worms will take a double dose of anti-change medication until further notice! It is imperative to remain calm; the situation is under control. Good night, and have an uneventful evening."

"And now, back to our regularly scheduled program," said the announcer.

Jumping up, Cathy switched off the TV.

"Hey! I was watchin' that!" said Fred.

Cathy ran to Charley's door and threw it open without knocking. She looked around and saw that all Charley's drawings had been torn off the walls, but there was no Charley. "Charley! Where are you?" she demanded. Charley's voice came from under the bed.

"I'm under here—trying to find my homework."

"Come out from under there right now!" said Cathy.

Finally Charley's red face emerged from under his bed. "Hi, Mom. What's for dinner?"

"Charley Littlefield! Did you *change* at school today?"

"Yeah, for soccer practice," he joked, knowing that lying would get him nowhere.

"There's no need to get smart, young man," said Cathy. "I want the whole story, and I want it now!"

Slowly Charley slid out of his hiding place, crawled up on the bed and let out a sigh. "I drew another picture, okay? And somebody finked on me. Mrs. Beige told me I'd have to stay after class and write, "A worm is a worm is a worm" a thousand more times. I told her I wasn't going to do it anymore, and that's when it happened," he said. "I'm sorry! I couldn't help it."

Cathy sat down beside her son on the bed and held her head in her hands. "We'll be lucky if they don't quarantine you," she said.

"I know," said Charley miserably. "I'm scared."

"We've got to hide you!" said Cathy. "But where?"

Just then came a *rat-ta-tat-tat!* at the window. Charley and his mother both jumped. "What was that?" said Cathy. Charley shook his head, his eyes big.

Rat-a-tat-tat! This time the sound was more urgent. Cathy went to the window and opened the curtains. Monique was hovering outside, the orange and blue of her wings lighting up the room like sunshine. She gave them a friendly smile and a little wave.

"Ahhhhh!" cried Cathy, jerking the curtains shut and jumping back a few feet. Charley rushed to the window and opened them again; Monique was still there.

"Please," she yelled through the window. Can you let me in for a minute? I'm lost!"

"Don't you dare," Cathy ordered, but Charley opened the window anyway and the butterfly flew in.

"Hi, I'm Monique," she said. "Do you have any nectar?"

"Wh-wh-wh…" Cathy stammered.

"You're so beautiful!" Charley blurted out.

"Thank you," said Monique, taking the compliment in stride. "I got trapped in this place by accident because I was being chased by humans, and now I just need directions as to how to get out, and a little nectar for the road, if you know what I mean."

"What's nectar?" asked Cathy suspiciously.

Monique stared at Cathy. "Seriously? You're kidding, right?" she asked. By now Monique was extremely thirsty. "I mean, there have to be a few flowers, or at least some milkweed, around somewhere. What do you guys eat?"

"Mostly a lot of dried wood," replied Cathy. "Sometimes we have mud pies for dessert."

"Oooh!" said Monique, making a face. "No wonder you're all still caterpillars. You're basically starving to death!"

"We're *worms*," not catapults—whatever you said," Charlie answered.

"Oh-kay," muttered Monique under her breath, realizing the conversation was going nowhere. "Thanks anyway!"

As she hopped toward the window, suddenly there was a loud "BOOM! BOOM! BOOM!" at the front door. Cathy clutched her heart with one hand. "That'll be the guards," said Charley.

"Stay here!" Cathy ordered him. "Hide under the bed! *You* can go," she said to Monique. Then she marched out of the room, slamming the door behind her.

Monique looked at Charley with real curiosity. "So what was the problem today, anyway?" she asked. "Is shedding your skin some kind of crime around here?"

"Yeah . . . that's exactly what it is," answered Charley. "But how did *you* know about that?"

"I saw you through the window of that—horrible place," said Monique. "Why do you have to go there?"

"Because we just do," said Charley. "Didn't you go to school?"

"Of course not! Why would I need to? All butterflies have to do is fly, drink nectar, migrate . . . and eventually, mate and have eggs, of course. But I'm putting that off for as long as possible," said Monique, brushing off her wings. "Well, it was nice meeting you!" she said, hopping toward the window.

BOOM! BOOM! BOOM! Again, the pounding at the door.

"Wait a minute," Charley said quickly. "Take me with you."

"Oh, I can't do that," said Monique. "How would you keep up with me? You're not even a very fast crawler. Sorry, but absolutely not!"

"Come on," Charley pleaded. "You don't exactly blend in around here! You've got to shake the guards, fast! You think you can out-fly those cockroaches? Some of them can jump ten feet! And you don't have any idea where the mouth of the cave is. I could help you get out."

Monique jumped on the windowsill. "I'll find it."

"Wait," said Charley. "I could ride on your back."

Monique sniffed. "I'm not a horse!"

"Listen, Miss, uh, Lady . . . if they catch me I'll be quarantined. Nobody knows for sure what happens to worms who change, but they never come home! I'll probably end up being some cockroach's dinner! I can get you back to the Outside World, I swear. *Please*!"

While Monique was thinking this over, Fred and Cathy were at the front door. Their unwanted guests were still pounding. BOOM! BOOM! BOOM!

"Open up, in the name of the queen," a husky voice yelled, "or we'll knock the door down!"

"Don't do it," Cathy begged Fred.

"We don't have any choice, honey," said Fred. He opened the door, and three giant cockroaches in brown uniforms barged in, knocking the door right off its hinges. "Is there a problem, officers?" asked Fred meekly.

"Where's the kid? The one who shed his skin today," snarled the largest one, backing Fred into a corner. "He's your son, ain't he?"

"Yes, sir, but he's feeling much better now," said Cathy. "He took a double dose of anti-change medication, and he'll be fine in the morning, I promise!"

"Oh, sure," said the guard sarcastically, sniffing around. "Once changed, never the same!"

In a flash one of the guards was at Charley's door. "Over here, sir!" he said.

"Break it down if you have to," said the head guard.

"No! You cannot take my son!" Cathy shrieked. In a flash she positioned herself between Charley's door and the guards. The head guard rudely grabbed her and flung her out of the way. Then he kicked the door in, and all three roaches scurried inside.

Charley's room was now empty. The head guard turned and glared at Cathy. "Where are you hiding him?" he demanded.

"I'm not! He—he—he was here just a minute ago," Cathy stammered.

The cockroaches did a quick search under the bed and in Charley's closet. "Hey! The window's open," said one of them, possibly the brightest of the three. "He probably went out that way."

"Sound the alarms!" the head guard ordered. "Come on!" All three cockroaches then jumped right over Cathy and darted out of the room.

Cathy rushed to the window and stared into the darkness. "Run, Charley! Run!" she whispered.

Chapter Three

"Wow! You can really fly!" Charley said to Monique, his excitement momentarily overriding his fear. Monique was now flying straight into the darkness of the cave, her young passenger gripping her tightly with all twelve of his arms and legs.

"Well, of course," Monique replied. "But I'm not going to be able to fly for very long, with you on my back. You're pretty heavy." At that moment a deafening alarm sounded, echoing from every corner of the cave.

"Geez, Louise! What was that?" asked Monique.

"It's the guards. Fly faster, can you?" Charley yelled.

"I'm flying as fast as I can," said Monique. "I can't see a thing. Which way should I go?"

"Uh—that way," said Charley. What Monique didn't know was that this was strictly a guess, since Charley had never been anywhere but to school and back in his whole life. He was giddy with the thrill of flying, but at the same time terrified of what was happening to him. Charley and all of his friends had grown up being told that "changing" was almost always fatal.

"Fine," said Monique, turning towards a part of the cave dotted with small, petrified trees. Perhaps enough rain and sunlight had once penetrated the cave's ceiling enough to give it some vegetation. "I'm going to have to stop and rest," Monique said breathlessly.

She alighted on a gnarly tree branch and looked over her shoulder at Charley, who hadn't relaxed his grip a bit. She cleared her throat. "You can get off now!" she told him.

Slowly, Charley loosened his grip on Monique, one leg at a time. "You're awesome! What kind of fly did you say you were again?"

Monique looked at Charley and decided he wasn't kidding. "A *butter*fly. That's what you're going to be, too," she said. "Probably very soon."

"I told you," said Charley sarcastically. "I'm a worm. A silkworm. And when I grow up, I'll go to work in the factory and spin silk for the queen, just like my parents, for the rest of my life." Monique said nothing, so Charley continued in a low voice. "I mean, I've always wanted to . . . fly. But I've never said it out loud."

"Then, say it! Say, 'I want to fly,'" she encouraged him. "No—'I'm *going* to fly.' Well, go ahead!"

Just then a searchlight flashed across the next tree, and they heard the scratchy sound of cockroach feet approaching from what sounded like just yards away.

"Come on!" We've got to scoot!" said Charley, jumping on Monique's back without being invited.

"Now, wait a minute," she said, shaking him off. "I told you, I can't carry you like this. I've got to get back to my flock, and you're slowing me down!"

"Please—I swear, I can help you find the way out. Don't leave me here!" Charley pleaded.

Monique sighed. The searchlight shot over their tree, this time barely missing them. "Oh, all right, get on. Hurry, before I change my mind!"

"Thanks! You won't be sorry," said Charley, hopping on her back. She lifted off just as two cockroach guards, Lieutenant White and Sergeant Field, got close enough to catch a glimpse of Monique's stunning wings.

"Holy mackerel! Did you see that?" Lieutenant White asked Field.

"Uh—I wasn't gonna say nothin', but if you saw it, I saw it," said the sergeant.

"After it, men!" White yelled. Field and a unit of cockroach guards obediently charged ahead, but Monique was already out of sight.

At this point, Martha the Moth-Queen had no idea that Charley had escaped with the help of a butterfly from the Outside World. If she had, she would have been far too upset to go back to her usual beauty regimen. She always applied a double-mud face mask with extra silk protein in the evening, after a meal of imported nectar and caviar. It never made her look any better, but all the guards told her it did. (If you've never seen a Death's-head moth wearing a double-mud face mask, try to avoid it.) She sat on her throne, which was actually just a large, wooden wheelchair covered with shiny bits of stalagmites for decoration. Martha spoke to her sickly-looking son Edgar, who was perched on a nearby stool reading *Mighty Moth* magazine.

"It's no fun getting old," she said, tossing her hand mirror aside.

"You still look pretty good for your age, Mother," yawned Edgar, turning a page.

"Oh, thank you so much, Edgar," mocked the queen. "I live for your compliments."

Outside, Lieutenant White and Sergeant Field marched grimly down the hallway. "Why do I have to tell her?" asked Field.

"Because it was your fault!" said White.

"*My* fault? How do you figure that?"

"Because you can run faster than I can. It was your fault," said White.

"That ain't fair," Field complained. "Let's tell her together, you know, at the same time."

"Fine," said White. "We'll do it on the count of three." Having reached the Queen's quarters, he cleared his throat. "Request permission to enter, Your Majesty!"

"Permission granted!" said Martha.

The curtains parted, and Lieutenant White and Sergeant Field entered, bowing and kowtowing. "Long live the queen!" they said in unison.

"Where is the worm?" Martha snapped.

"One . . . two . . . three," said White under his breath, elbowing Field. "He got away!" White declared. Field held his tongue.

"*WHAT DID YOU SAY?*" Martha screamed.

"I didn't say nothin', Your Majesty, it was him," said Field with a nauseating grin.

"Why, I oughta—" began White, his hands around Field's neck.

"Lieutenant! You are in charge, and I demand an explanation for your incompetence! Now!"

"Well, there was this b-b-beautiful orange-and-blue insect with wings, and she p-p-picked the kid up right in front of us, and then flew away."

Field jumped in, suddenly eager to tell the story. "I mean, you should've seen her, Your Ladyhood. Whatever she was, she was gorgeous! I mean, unbelievable! Prince Edgar, sir, between you and me— holy cow!" he said, adding a wolf whistle.

At this the queen's eyes bulged to twice their normal size. "A

gorgeous orange-and-blue insect with wings," she purred, her voice much calmer than her expression. "That appeared to fly. My goodness, that's something you don't see every day!"

"No, ma'am," said Field, "No, it sure as heck ain't."

"Did you hear that, Edgar?" Queen Martha asked. "Quite interesting, isn't it?"

"Yes, it is, Mother," replied Edgar, who looked as though he might drool. "It certainly is."

"And she got the kid, and flew away, into the cave!" Lieutenant White burst out. "There was no way we could catch 'em!" Perhaps unwisely, he added, "May I be eaten alive by bats if I'm lyin'!"

"That's right! We tried, believe me," Sergeant Field went on. "What were we gonna do—they could fly, and we couldn't! It wasn't for lack of tryin'. I mean, that flying thing was a real looker!"

At this, the queen's mud mask broke off, revealing her ugly, wrinkled face and scaring the life out of White and Field.

"I mean, her wings were kind of gaudy . . . "

"Garish!"

"Way too much!" they agreed.

Edgar then whipped out a photograph he'd been hiding in his magazine. "Did she look anything like this?" he asked innocently. It was a picture of a monarch butterfly, a beautiful young female who bore a striking resemblance to Monique, but with regular orange-and-black wings.

"That's her!" exclaimed White and Field in unison.

"Edgar!" said the queen. "Give that to me this instant!"

Edgar eyed his mother and for a moment considered disobeying her, the devil with the consequences. But at last he gave in and handed it over. Instantly the queen popped the picture into her mouth and swallowed it whole. "You were saying, officers?" she asked with a toothless smile.

At this unseemly behavior, White gulped. "I'm sorry, Your Majesty, but they flew away, and we ran after 'em as long as we could, but before long we couldn't see 'em any more, and . . . and . . ."

"*ONLY THE QUEEN AND HER SON CAN FLY!*" Martha bellowed.

"Y-y-yes, Your Holiness, we know that, of course," said White. "Only the queen and her son can fly. He just meant that it *looked* like it was flying. Of course, it didn't fly—that would be ridiculous! No way. No how. Negatory. Nuh-uh," said White, making use of his extensive vocabulary.

"Now hear me, you impudent nincompoops," said Martha, regaining her composure and pausing for dramatic effect. "The only creatures who have been given the gift of flight are our royal self, Prince Edgar, and the royal horseflies. No other creature can, or will ever be allowed to, fly. *IS THAT UNDERSTOOD?*"

"Yes, yes, Your Majesty," White responded, trembling.

"Uh, can we go now?" asked Field.

The queen spat. "Yes, you lamebrain, you may go! You will catch the kidnapper and the sick child by midnight tomorrow night, on pain of death! And it won't be a quick death. It will be a slow, painful death, to be administered by Prince Edgar himself. Isn't that right, Edgar?"

"Iccccch," said Edgar. "Do I have to?"

"Don't let him fool you," laughed the queen. "Edgar loves nothing better than a lunch of roasted cockroaches now and then. Quite the treat for him, actually! Now repeat after me. *'I swear on my honor'* . . ."

"I swear on my honor," White and Field intoned.

"To deliver the creature and the worm . . ."

"To deliver the creature and the worm . . ."

"To the queen by midnight tomorrow night, or face slow and painful execution."

"To the queen by midnight tomorrow, or face slow and painful—

"Here Field broke off. "I don't want to die! I don't want to die!" he cried, grabbing White around the waist.

"Now, get out of my sight!" the queen roared.

"Now, get out of my sight!" chanted the still-hypnotized White.

At this, Queen Martha let out an ear-splitting shriek that would have awakened the dead. The cockroach guards turned and fled from the room in terror. Edgar looked at his mother, amused. "Oh I don't know, Mommy Dearest, I think you were a bit hard on them," he said.

"On the contrary, I'm just being a good monarch—get it?" she answered smugly. "And where did you get that photograph? Hmmm?"

"Oh, I—don't know, I—found it somewhere," he said vaguely. "You know, was thinking—perhaps I should go in search of the creature myself. The guards will undoubtedly screw it up."

"Edgar, I'm so touched!" said the queen, her voice dripping with sarcasm. "Would you really do that for me? You know how much I'd love to own a pair of real butterfly wings, don't you?"

"Absolutely, Mother dear, anything for you! If you want those wings, you shall have them!" said Edgar, a bit too quickly.

"Oh, cut the crap, son," said Martha. "I know what you're thinking. You want a bride—a *butterfly* bride. But unfortunately, that's not in the cards for you, not now, not ever! You will be king one day, and that will be enough. Moths do not marry butterflies. Understood?"

Edgar turned beet red. "It hadn't even crossed my mind," he said.

"Don't *ever* lie to me!" Martha threatened. "Take the horseflies, and bring me that creature, dead or alive. But watch that you don't damage her wings. The slightest tear, and they're ruined. I want them in perfect condition!"

"Absolutely, Mother," Edgar said as he flew to the door. "You will have them by midnight tomorrow night."

"Wait a minute, dear," she said. "Aren't we forgetting something?"

Edgar grudgingly circled back and gave his mother a peck on the cheek.

"That's better," she said. "Now be a good boy, and get going!"

So Edgar left the castle by himself for the first time in his life, overjoyed at the prospect of a day's freedom. The possibility of finding the beautiful butterfly was almost too much to hope for, but secretly he believed that if he caught her, eventually he could convince her to marry him. After all, his mother couldn't live forever.

"I've had about enough of being a good boy, Mummy dearest," Edgar muttered to himself on his way to the royal horseflies' nest. "I'm ready to be a *king*."

Chapter Four

By this time, Monique and Charley had put considerable distance between themselves and Queen Martha's castle. With Charley on her back, however, Monique had to stop and rest every few minutes. The alarming thing was that they could see no light coming from the direction they were headed in, or from any other direction, except for the few small holes in the roof of the cave. And they were much too high for Monique to have any hope of reaching them, especially with Charley on her back.

After an hour or more of this stop-and-go progress, they heard a piercing shriek in the distance.

"What was that?" asked Charley.

"Sounded like a bat," said Monique.

"What's a bat?"

"Bats are big, black, nasty flying things with sharp teeth."

"Great," said Charley. "Getting quarantined is sounding better all the time."

"Charley," said Monique. "If you don't stop complaining, you're going to have to walk the rest of the way."

"Okay, okay!" said Charley.

"I mean, seriously, I've got to get back, pronto," Monique continued. "My flock's in the middle of migration, and I don't know if they'll wait for me!"

"What's 'migration'?" asked Charley.

"It means we're going to Mexico for the winter. Whoa! Look at that!" Monique had just spotted a small pond directly below them. Doing an elegant swan dive, she landed just inches away from it. Charley rolled off her back with a moan.

"Ow! Give me a little more notice next time, would ya?"

"Stay here," said Monique. "I'll be back in a minute."

"Where are you going?" asked Charley.

"To see if there's anything to drink," Monique yelled over her shoulder. "Where there's water, there could be flowers. Daisies, dandelions, I'm not picky at this point!"

"What am I supposed to eat?" Charley asked.

Monique didn't answer. The truth was, at that moment all she could think of was her own hunger. She was already scouring the pond for some kind of nectar. She knew that in a pinch she could drink muddy water, but was hoping it wouldn't come to that.

"Okay, don't worry about me!" Charley called after her irritably. (Being hungry makes everybody irritable.) He looked around and saw some crabgrass near the pool's edge. He took a bite. "Not bad!" he admitted, and began to eat.

Flying over the pond, Monique noticed a good-sized rock jutting out of the middle. She landed on it, looked around and sighed. Not a single flower anywhere in sight. She extended her nose into the murky water and took a cautious sip. "Yeccch!" she said, spitting it out. Then she thought better of it. She sipped again, and this time gulped it down. Monique was beginning to wonder if she would ever have anything better than muddy water to drink. Circling the pool again, she hovered over it to see if she could catch a glimpse of her reflection, but the water was too dark. Instead she saw a small green lily pad, almost directly beneath her. "Oh, my gosh!" she said, landing on it. "Where there's a lily pad, there might be—"

At that moment she heard a loud "RIBBIT." Jerking her head around, she was confronted with the bulging eyes of a huge frog.

"Uh . . . hi there, I was just leaving," she said. But before she could even flap her wings once, the frog hurled out its tongue and caught her on the first try. "Ahhh!!! Let go of me!" she squealed as the frog sucked her into his mouth.

"Let me out of here, or you'll be sorry!" Monique screamed at the top of her lungs from inside the frog. "Monarchs are poisonous to frogs, no kidding! HEEEELLPP!!"

At this, the frog's cheeks swelled up to ten times their normal size, and he looked like he was going to be sick. Then he opened his mouth wide and hurled Monique out along with a lot of vile, gooey stuff. The whole mess shot onto a rock in the middle of the pond.

"Told you," Monique said to the frog, wiping her face. The frog managed another weak "Ribbit," and hopped away. "Yuck! Disgusting!" said Monique, taking a quick bath in the water. She shook herself off and made it back to the shore, looking more like a pitiful, wilted flower than a butterfly. "Charley?" she called out. "Where are you?"

"Over here!" said Charley's voice.

He emerged from a tall clump of grass, looking twice as big as he had been just ten minutes before.

"What happened to you? You're huge!" said Monique.

"You told me to eat," Charley reminded her. He belched informally. "Did you find any flowers?"

"No, I didn't any find any flowers. Just some muddy water and a giant frog who almost ate me, in case you're interested."

"What's a frog?" asked Charley.

Monique looked at him, unamused. "I take it back. You do need to go to school, and we're going to find one for you as soon as we get out of here."

"*If* we ever get out of here," Charley sighed. He was starting to feel guilty about having left his mom and dad, because he knew they'd be worried. He looked at the cave's seemingly endless, dark expanse. "Do you think the Outside World is that way?"

Monique almost choked. Charley had promised he knew the way out! But she decided to let it drop for now, and said only, "Let's get going." Charley waddled over to her and threw his arms and legs around her torso. Attempting lift-off, Monique immediately fell back on the ground with a thud.

"Oh, my gosh! This isn't going to work. You're going to have to walk, my friend!"

"Walk!" Charley repeated. "With you flying? I can't keep up with you!" "Then I'll fly slower," she said, ungrammatically.

"But that'll take forever!"

"It's our only choice. Either that, or we can wait here until you change, and then you can fly on your own. From the looks of you, that shouldn't be long."

Until now, Charley had thought Monique must be fibbing about his potential to become a butterfly, just to make him feel better. But something about the way she said it this time made him think that she meant it.

"You really think I'm going to be a butterfly—don't you?" he asked, peering at her closely.

Monique let out an exasperated sigh. "Yes, yes, a thousand times yes! You're a caterpillar. After you pop out of your cocoon, you *will* fly—it's the most natural thing in the world."

"What's a cocoon?" asked Charley.

Monique sighed, trying to be patient. "It's a hard shell of a thing that you make for yourself when you're ready to change. Don't worry, it happens to everybody. The old 'you' sort of . . . melts, and in a few days—*voila*! You come out, a butterfly."

"*Melts?*" Charley thought. He sat there, trying to comprehend what Monique was saying without feeling like a fool. As they continued to talk, Lieutenant White and Sergeant Field peeked out from behind a nearby boulder. They had been following Monique and Charley for some time.

"There they are!" White whispered.

"Yeah," said Field, licking his lips at the sight of Monique. "Boy, she's pretty."

"But if the queen asks—"

"She's ugly," replied Field.

"As a mud fence! Now, when I say go, you bag the kid, and I'll get the beautiful flying thing," White instructed.

"Why do you get to go for the beautiful flying thing?" Field asked.

"Because I'm the one with the net, knucklehead! You've got a wittle bag, for the wittle worm!"

They began crawling through the grass. They were within inches of their prey when Monique finally looked up. White and Field froze.

"Hold on! I saw something moving," she said to Charley.

Charley looked around. "I don't see anything."

"Well, anyway, we should get going," said Monique. "What do you think about that-a-way?

"Fine with me," said Charley. "I mean, yeah—that way!" Charley began walking, Monique looping in lazy circles above him. Suddenly White and Field emerged from the grass behind them and started half-running, half-hopping toward them. Charley saw them first and let out a yell.

"Monique! It's the guards!" he yelled, trying to move faster.

"Stop in the name of the queen!" Field hollered, flailing at Charley with the bag. Monique landed, bravely planting herself between Charley and the cockroaches. She spread her wings and struck a pose.

"Hello, officers! Can I help you?" she asked the cockroaches, who had stopped dead in their tracks. "Run!" she whispered to Charley.

"Well, hello, ma'am," said Field. "You sure are lookin' nice today!"

White broke out in a cold sweat. He knew the queen had threatened him with certain death if he came back to the castle empty-handed, but even though he told his arms to raise the net and trap Monique, he couldn't do it.

"You new to these parts?" he asked her instead.

"As a matter of fact, I am," said Monique, batting her eyes. "You gentlemen wouldn't know how to help a girl get back to the Outside World, would you?"

"Well, uh, unfortunately, we've got orders to, uh . . . ." White broke off.

"To do what?" Monique smiled. She continued to draw out the conversation, giving Charley a chance to escape. He was now crawling as fast as he could, but the floor of the cave was very uneven and rocky. Suddenly something caught one of Charley's back legs and he tripped, rolling into a shallow hole. Exhausted and out of breath, he decided to wait for Monique to catch up. But he was so sleepy that soon it was impossible to keep his eyes open. "I've got to stay awake until she finds me," he thought to himself. Within seconds, he was sound asleep.

The next morning, the "grown-up" caterpillars were at the factory, spinning silk for Queen Martha as usual. Each caterpillar crawled inside a wheel that shot out brightly colored threads that attached themselves to the other caterpillars' work in a huge, constantly growing ball at the front of the factory.

Cathy Littlefield stared into space as she worked, her six feet barely turning her wheel. "You're way behind, Cath," whispered Fred. "You're gonna get a ticket!"

"He got away," Cathy muttered to herself. "At least he got away!"

The factory boss, a huge cockroach, cracked a whip. "Faster! Faster!" he yelled. Suddenly the loudspeaker squealed, and Queen Martha herself appeared on a large screen hanging from the rafters. "Listen up, worms!" yelled the boss, and the caterpillars stopped spinning.

"Citizens of Wormland! Last night a dangerous alien creature entered the kingdom and abducted the young worm with changing fever before he could be quarantined," Martha began.

The workers began to mumble amongst themselves. Again the boss screamed: "Quiet!"

"Any worm with knowledge of their whereabouts is hereby ordered to report it immediately," Martha continued. "Furthermore, any worm caught aiding or abetting the fugitives in any way will be arrested and imprisoned without a trial. Carry on." The screen went black.

Back at her station, Cathy looked at Fred. *Poisonous!?*" she cried out. She jumped off her wheel and ran for the door. Her husband intercepted her before she got there.

"Sorry, officer, everything's fine," Fred assured him.

"No, it isn't," Cathy moaned. "It's my son that's missing! My baby's been kidnapped by a poisonous alien! Doesn't anybody care?"

"Let me think. Nope!" said the factory boss. "Now back to work!"

Cathy stared at her caterpillar comrades, who looked away and fidgeted nervously. Fred put his arm around her.

"Come on, honey," he said gently, and walked her back to her post.

About this time, Charley was waking up from a lovely dream. He had dreamed that he was already a butterfly, zipping around from poppy to pansy and having a grand old time. When he opened his eyes and found himself in the same damp hole he'd fallen asleep in the night before, his heart sank. He crawled out of the hole and looked around.

"What now?" His voice echoed back to him: *"WHAT NOW WHAT NOW WHAT NOW?"*

"We keep going," said a voice behind him, the cave adding, *"KEEP GOING KEEP GOING KEEP GOING!"* Charley spun around and saw Monique's orange-and-blue wings flap once on the ground a few feet away.

"Monique!" said Charley, running over to her. "I thought I'd lost you!"

"I knew you couldn't have gone far," said Monique, stretching her wings. "Oooh—boy, I'm sore!" she moaned.

"But what about the guards? How'd you get rid of them?" Charley asked.

"Um, I told them I'd try to teach them how to fly, and they were jumping up and down all over the place. After a while, they got so dizzy they passed out."

"Awesome! But shouldn't we get going? They'll come after us when they wake up," said Charley.

"Give me a minute," said Monique, who was grouchy from not getting enough sleep. "I've got to get my bearings. Hey—what's that over there?" Charley looked in the direction where Monique was pointing. It definitely looked like the cave was lighter over that way.

"It's the Outside World! Let's go," Charley said, jumping on Monique's back.

"Ugh!" said Monique, collapsing on her stomach with a *splat*. "Are you kidding me? I can't achieve lift-off with a five-pound caterpillar on my back!"

"Oh, yeah," said Charley, and dismounted. "Sorry."

"Don't worry about it," Monique said, feeling a little guilty. Again they set off, Monique flying slowly in figure-8's above Charley, who did his best to keep up.

They had been circling through the cave like this for what seemed like hours when Monique saw something up ahead of them. Actually, she smelled it before she saw it, her antennae standing straight up. "What's that?" she asked.

"You mean that smell?" asked Charley.

"Yeah! Smells like nectar!"

Straight ahead of them was a windowless shack big enough for a human. It had a chimney from which a curl of smoke was escaping. On the door was a small, crudely written sign: "ROYAL NECTAR BANK. KEEP OUT!"

"What does that say?" Monique demanded.

"Can't you read?" asked Charley.

"I'm a butterfly, why would I need to?"

"So . . . maybe I'm not so dumb after all. Right?"

Charley waited, feeling good about himself for a change. "I never said you were dumb!" Monique said, although she knew she had been a little hard on Charley. "What does it say?"

"It says . . . 'royal nectar bank,'" Charley answered proudly.

"Nectar *bank*?" Monique exploded. "For real?"

"That's what it says," said Charley. "I guess the queen drinks nectar, too."

"But a whole bank of it? Just for *her*? Whew! Talk about selfish!"

Suddenly the front door swung open, and the maddeningly sweet smell of nectar came floating out like clouds of perfume. "Ahhhhh!" sighed Monique, closing her eyes. "I'm going in. Wait here!"

"No way!" said Charley. But before he reached the door, Monique shot out like a bullet, followed by a dozen leaping cockroach guards.

Lt. White and Sgt. Field had set fire to some rotting oranges, turning the ramshackle hut into a butterfly trap! White screamed at his men as he led the chase: "After 'em! Our necks are on the line!" Some of the guards swiped at Charley with their nets, while others jumped up and down, trying to scoop up Monique.

"Monique! Wait for me!" cried Charley, running as fast as an extremely chubby caterpillar can run. Monique hesitated, then doubled back and hovered just inches above him.

"Jump!" she yelled.

"I can't make it," said Charley, the cockroaches nipping at his heels. "You've got to land!"

"If I land, they'll catch me, too," said Monique. "Jump!" So Charley jumped, and by some miracle was able to grab Monique's tail end with a single "hand." She made a face and tried to gain altitude. Field in turn grabbed onto Charley's hindquarters.

"I've got 'em!" cried Field triumphantly. "Look at me, I'm flying!" And for a moment the butterfly, caterpillar and cockroach formed an unlikely circus act.

"Shake him off!" Monique ordered Charley, struggling to stay in the air. She flapped her wings violently, and at the same time Charley shook his tail with all his might. Finally Field fell to the ground with a *splat*!

"Yes!" exulted Charley, still dangling precariously. "Bye, you big bullies! Nyah, nyah, nyah, nyah, nyah!"

"Get that worm!" White screamed at the guards, visions of his own execution dancing in his head. The army of cockroaches hopped after their prey, but Monique and Charley were out of sight.

Chapter Five

After this extremely close call, Monique flew on for a few minutes, not daring to stop or even look back. Charley kept his eyes shut and gripped her as tightly as he could. "Monique—I can't hold on much longer!" he said.

"Neither can I!" she said. She had been flying on pure adrenaline until now, and as soon as she thought about it, Charlie's weight began pulling her down like a lead balloon. She stopped flapping her wings and dropped straight down to the floor of the cave at an almost perpendicular angle. "Okay, let go of me. *Please*," she added.

"You were incredible back there," Charley said shyly when his feet touched the ground.

"All I want to do is sleep," sighed Monique, ignoring the compliment. "But I guess we'd better keep going till we're sure we've lost them."

"Okay," sighed Charley, and started crawling. Monique hopped beside him, her energy almost gone. She shivered; her wings were getting cold. She knew that if she didn't get out of the cave soon, her body temperature would drop so low that she wouldn't be able to fly at all.

"Hey—what's that over there?"

To their left, against the wall of the cave, was a long wooden structure that resembled a miniature barn. "Maybe we can stop there for a nap if it's empty," she said. "At least we'd be protected from bats. Wait here while I check it out."

"I'm going with you," Charley insisted.

"Suit yourself," said Monique. As they cautiously approached the barn, they saw two large cockroach guards sitting outside the door, snoozing. "Rats!" said Monique. "Hide over there behind that rock and watch them like a hawk. If they wake up, holler!" This time, Charley did as he was told.

Summoning all her strength, Monique flew up to the roof and looked in through the barn's one tiny window. What she saw shocked her: dozens of delicate butterflies in wire cages, sitting on top of their eggs like chickens. They looked weak, tired and hungry. One of the butterflies moaned as the pile of eggs below her grew higher.

"Oooh! That's it—I'm done," she said with an exhausted groan.

"I'm so thirsty," said another.

"If you lick your lips, it helps a little," said another.

Horrified, Monique tried to get their attention. "Psst!" The butterflies looked up and saw what from their point of view, looked like an enormous butterfly. With a little gasp, one of them spoke up. "What are you doing here?"

"Shh! Don't wake the guards," Monique whispered. "I was going to ask you the same thing."

The butterflies glanced at each other. Then Jenny, the one who'd spoken first, decided to trust Monique. "Ever since we changed," she said. "They quarantined us, and now we're egg-laying slaves."

"But why?" asked Monique. "What do they do with all those eggs?"

"The queen always needs more," shrugged a tired, yellow butterfly. "She makes caviar out of some of them, and the rest get adopted by the older caterpillars. They're so naive, they don't even know why they can't have kids themselves."

As Monique tried to comprehend how anyone could do such a thing, she tried to think of something to say that would make the butterflies feel better. "That 'queen' isn't a real queen," she said finally. "Apparently she's just a moth who's got everybody fooled! I don't understand why the caterpillars obey her. If there's anything I can do for you . . . "

At that moment the door of the barn flew open and the cockroach guards entered. "Egg check!" they announced. The butterfly prisoners sat at attention. The guards began checking each cage, counting the eggs each one had laid. Monique quietly flew off the roof of the cage, careful not to create any wind by flapping her wings, and glided back to the rock where Charley was hiding. "Come on, Charley. Let's go," she said.

"What's going on in there?" he asked.

"One day I'll tell you," said Monique. "Right now, let's find shelter and get some sleep."

"Hey, Monique," Charley said. "I need to tell you something." Monique waited. "I don't really know the way out. I just said I did to get you to take me with you."

"I already knew," Monique said gently.

"And if we don't make it, I—"

"Don't even say that," she told him. "We're getting out of here. Both of us, do you hear?" She looked around. "I think it's lighter over there." Too tired to fly, she resumed hopping, with Charley following close behind.

Meanwhile, White, Field and the rest of the guards continued what they now believed to be a futile search. "Here, Charley! Here, Charley," Field called out listlessly.

"He's not a dog, you blockhead," said White.

They trudged on in silence. At last the cockroaches came upon a rotting pile of garbage. "Lieutenant! Request permission for a rest stop!" said one of the guards.

"Okay," answered White. "Ten minutes, tops!" The insects pounced on the putrid pile and began devouring it. White sat down and watched them, his appetite suddenly gone. "What's the use? We're never going to find them now," he muttered.

Field, who was enjoying what was left of an old shoe, heard the shriek first. A very large, black bat was headed straight for them! "B-B-B—" Field stammered, pointing at a spot behind White's head.

"What?" White asked. "Spit it out." But all Field could do was stutter and stare. White turned around and saw the thing, its mouth wide open and ready for the kill. "AHHHHH!" he screamed, and dived under a pile of leaves. The bat made a sharp right turn and zeroed in on the garbage heap and its diners.

"BAT! BAT!" Field yelled to the others, who froze, then scattered. Field zigzagged every which way as the creature swiped at him, barely missing each time. Making it to a smaller pile of leaves, Field jumped in. The bat flapped its wings and saw a line of cockroaches running for their lives in the other direction. He caught up to them, picking off one, then another, then another, and popping them in his mouth like popcorn. Finally he vanished.

After a few seconds, White's pile of leaves rustled. He peeked out cautiously. Feeling strangely courageous, he hurried over to the garbage mound and started gnawing on an ancient apple core. The other leaf pile rustled and Field emerged, trembling. "Lieutenant! You're alive!" He rushed over, flung himself into White's arms and sobbed.

"Get a-hold of yourself," White grumbled, pushing him away.

"I can't go on!" cried Field. "I can't!"

White opened his mouth to say something, then immediately shut it. Suddenly he couldn't think of a single reason to keep going, either.

"Let's forget about the kid!" Field went on. "Forget about the flying creature! Let's just get while the gettin's good," he begged.

"You know what? I'm done, too," said White. "But this means we're *never* going back! We're AWOL. Finished. Kaput. Deal?"

"Yes, sir! Yes, sir! Deal, deal, deal!" Field saluted so many times that White finally had to shake him. And the cockroaches marched on, the moth-queen's servants no longer.

At that moment Prince Edgar was prowling the cave with six of his royal horseflies, searching for signs of Monique and Charley. Edgar hadn't been allowed outside the castle in ages, and frankly he was having quite a time of it. "I am Prince Edgar," he sang as he flew. "All who see me fear me!"

"You are Prince Edgar," the horseflies sang back. "All who see you fear you!"

"Only I can fly, can fly!"

"Only you can fly, can fly," repeated the horseflies (although obviously they could fly, too).

"I am lord of all I survey!"

"You are lord of all you survey!"

"And I am going to be king one day!"

"And you are going to be king one day!"

Now feeling completely full of himself, Edgar began laughing. "Ha ha ha ha ha ha," he laughed in a sing-song tone, until the horseflies felt obliged to join in, their fake laughter echoing throughout the cave. Edgar continued humming to himself cheerily for a while, but he'd been flying for what seemed like hours without a glimpse of so much as an ant. His hum got quieter and quieter and finally stopped.

"Well, where the devil are they?" he bellowed.

"Perhaps they've been killed by bats, sir," said one of the horseflies. "The cave is full of them."

"Nonsense! They're either hiding, or they've found some ally who has helped them escape. I say—it's getting annoyingly bright in here. Say, what's that up ahead?"

They had indeed been getting closer and closer to the cave's mouth, and Edgar wasn't used to the light. In the distance, he could see a long rock wall that formed a line all the way from one side of the cave to the other.

"It's No-No Land, sir. The queen declared it off limits many years ago. Perhaps we should turn back," said one of the flies.

"Don't worry about it," answered Edgar. "My mother just named it that to keep the worms from getting too close to the mouth of the cave. For princes, nothing is off-limits."

"Very good, sir," said the horsefly.

"I've always wanted an adventure, and now, I am having one," Edgar said grandly. "Shall we, officers?"

And the horseflies flew a bit faster, careful to let Edgar keep the lead.

About this time Monique and Charley were waking up from having slept far longer than they meant to. Just a few minutes after leaving the butterfly prison, they had come upon an old water pipe and crawled inside for a nap.

"Ugh," Monique groaned, opening one eye and stretching her wings. "Is this really my life?" Her voice reverberated oddly inside the pipe.

Next to her, Charley was talking in his sleep. "Woo! Ahh! Weee!" (He was having another flying dream.)

"Wake up," said Monique, tapping him on the shoulder. "We've gotta go."

Charley opened his eyes and, realizing that he was still a caterpillar, sighed. "I'm hungry," he said.

"Tell me about it," said Monique. Then her antennae perked up and she motioned to Charley to stay quiet. There were voices outside.

"I'm completely turned around," they heard Sgt. Field say. "Which way do we go?"

"I don't know. Shut up and let me think!" said Lt. White.

"Hey—what's that over there?"

Monique hopped to the end of the pipe and peeked out. She could see White and Field just a few feet away with their backs to her. They were very close to the rock wall that Edgar and the flies had just spotted from the air.

"I dunno," said White. "It could be No-No Land."

"No-No Land!" said Field excitedly. "Ain't that where Carny Town is? I hear it's unbelievable! Dancing girls! Gambling! All the food you can eat! Hallelujah, this is our lucky day!" He took off running, but White caught him by one leg and yanked him back.

"Now listen," said White. "No-No Land is off-limits for cockroaches, pretty much for everybody. It's at the very edge of the cave, that's why the queen doesn't let anybody go there."

"What queen? You mean Martha the ugly moth?" said Field, and laughed hysterically.

"Get over yourself, sergeant!" said White. "Hey—we should change our names, to be on the safe side. We can't let on that we were royal guards. I'll be Rocco; suits me better," he said, flexing a muscle.

"Okay, I'll be . . . Dexter," said Field.

"Dexter! What kind of a name is that? I'll call you Ricky."

"But what if I don't like Ricky?" asked Field.

"Tricky Ricky! Ha ha ha!" White laughed. "It's perfect. Come on, Carny Town's waitin' for us."

Field, or Ricky, didn't much like being told what to do, but he was too anxious to get to Carny Town to argue. So Rocco and Ricky scampered off toward what they were sure would be a dream vacation.

Monique turned to Charley, her face glowing. "You heard them," she grinned. "We're almost at the end of the cave! Come on!" Monique flew out of the pipe and saw the wall that White and Field had been discussing, which was the only thing now separating her from freedom. Just beyond it, Charley could see the first real sunlight of his life.

Chapter Six

Cathy and Fred Littlefield were now marching to the factory, about to begin their shift. Cathy had spent another sleepless night worrying about what might have happened to Charley.

"Fred!" she whispered to her husband. "What do you think about what they said yesterday?" she asked.

"What do you mean? About Charley gettin' abducted by a poisonous—"

"Shh! Not so loud," she said, cutting him off. Some of the other caterpillars in line glanced at them nervously.

"I don't know. I don't believe in aliens," Fred said quietly.

"Neither do I!" said Cathy. "Hey, Norman! Hey, Wilma! I've got to tell you something," she blurted out to the couple in front of her. "My son did not get abducted by an alien. He escaped, with the help of a beautiful creature with wings! It could fly, too, just like the queen! I'm telling you, I saw it with my own eyes!"

"Ha ha ha!" Fred said loudly as they walked past a cockroach guard. "My wife is such a kidder! Always trying to put a good face on things!"

"No, I'm not!" said Cathy. "It's the truth! Doesn't anybody care?"

But the others said nothing, too afraid to speak up. They simply marched into the silk factory as usual, got on their spinning wheels, and began another day of laboring for a selfish queen who made their lives miserable. To Cathy, it now made no sense at all.

At the same moment, "Rocco and Ricky" were approaching the entrance to Carny Town as fast as they could hop. A bug-sized billboard read: "CARNY TOWN 30 FEET AHEAD!" And the next: "CARNY TOWN 20 FEET AHEAD!" And so on. White and Field started running as they could, because the smells on the other side of the wall promised a tantalizing feast of hot dogs, hamburgers, cotton candy, caramel apples and other treats they'd only heard of but never tasted.

After a few minutes they came to a hole in the middle of the wall with a small ticket-taker's booth outside. A sign said "ADMISSION 5 SENTS." Never having seen a ticket-taker's booth, the roaches proceeded to hop right past it. A tall Granddaddy Longlegs jumped out of the booth, blocking their path and towering over them.

"Hold it right there, guys! You gotta buy a ticket," he said.

"Okay," said White, staring up at the Daddy Longlegs. "Here's five cents."

"Uh—that was yesterday," said the insect, quickly crossing out the "5 Sents" and changing it to "5 Dollers."

"You can't do that!" fumed White.

"Looks like I just did," smiled the Longlegs.

"I'll give you 10 cents," said White.

"One dollar," bargained the ticket-taker.

"That's highway robbery! Here—but that's for both of us," said White, and pulled out a bill.

"Gentlemen, enjoy yourselves." The Granddaddy Longlegs grinned and disappeared back inside the booth.

Watching this scene from behind a nearby rock were Monique and Charley. They looked at each other. "Do you smell what I smell?" asked Monique.

"Yeah, I know," said Charley. "Nectar."

"Or something very close to it," said Monique. "You stay here while I check it out."

"I'm not waiting out here by myself," Charley said stubbornly.

"Well, we don't have any money. How are you going to get past *that*?" Monique pointed at the ticket booth.

"We could dig a tunnel under the wall, and get in that way," said Charley.

"Hmm, dig a tunnel for you when all I have to do is fly over," answered Monique. "Doesn't make a lot of sense, my friend. Like I said: I'll fly over the wall, get us some food, and be right back. Anyways, it looks like you're going to cocooning soon, and after that you'll be able to fly out of the cave without any help from me!"

"Never mind," said Charley, annoyed. "You fly—I'll dig. I'll meet you on the other side.

Monique sighed. "Whatever," she said, preparing for take-off. All she could think about was the smell of that nectar.

"Hey, Monique, wait!" said Charley.

"What is it, Charley?"

"Don't leave the cave without me—okay?"

"I won't. I promise," said Monique.

Just then some new customers, a family of roly-poly bugs, approached the entrance to Carny Town. While the Daddy Longlegs was taking their money, Monique darted over the wall. Charley ran to the fence and started digging as fast as he could, throwing dirt every which way. Within seconds, he had vanished.

Inside Carny Town, White and Field were already having the time of their lives. They passed row after row of exhibits, each booth more colorful than the last. *"Right this way!"* called the barkers. *"See the Fat Lady! Fifteen unbelievable pounds of fat!"* *"Over here, fellas, see the incredible Five-Headed Bug!"* *"Funhouse! Funhouse! Get all the fun you need right here!"*

The cockroaches crawled on until they came to the Shooting Gallery, which looked to be far and away the most popular booth. Insects of all kinds had lined up to wait their turn. A customer raised his gun, took a shot and nailed a wooden bird. "Yeah! Got that sucker!" he bragged to the crowd.

"Wow! I'd like to shoot a bird," said Field.

"Who wouldn't?" said White. "But we should save our money for food. Hey—check *that* place out!"

Directly across from the Shooting Gallery was a café furnished with brightly colored tables and balloons, and a small stage on the far end. The cockroaches picked an empty table and a chubby waitress (a June bug) instantly appeared.

"Vhat'll you have?" she asked in a strange accent.

"What have you got?" asked White.

"Vhat do you vant?"

"How about a steak?"

"Ve ain't got steak."

"How about chicken?"

"Ve ain't got chicken."

"Well, what *do* you have?"

"I recommend de hash. Comes vith two sides," said the waitress.

"Sounds incredible," said White. "Surprise us!"

As the waitress waddled off, the stage lights came up and a small band of ants materialized. Four ladybugs in glittery costumes appeared and started jitterbugging to the music. When they saw that they had customers, they came out into the audience and danced right in front of the big-eyed White and Field. One of the ladies sat on Field's lap and gave him a little chuck under the chin.

"Hi there! I'm Ricky," said Field. (He had no idea that the dancing girls were expecting a very big tip.)

Meanwhile, Monique was flying over Carny Town, sniffing desperately for nectar or any kind of sugary liquid. But so far all she had seen were hot dog and hamburger stands, and a butterfly can't eat meat, even in an emergency. She was starting to believe that she would literally die of thirst when finally she smelled something that caused her to freeze in mid-air. Directly below her was a pink cotton candy stand! And although she'd never heard of cotton candy, the gooey substance smelled heavenly. She flew lower and hovered in front of it.

"Hello! Is anybody here?"

A hairy black spider emerged slowly from behind the booth, one hairy leg at a time. "Can I help you?" he asked in a low, gravelly voice.

"Um, one of those, please," said Monique, pointing an antenna at a cotton candy cone.

"Coming right up, lovely," said the spider. "I'm Spud, by the way. That'll be ten cents."

"Oh! I don't have any money," she said. "But I'm so thirsty, and—and—I just have to have some, or I really might die. Please, Mr. Spud!"

"No money, huh?" said Spud, suddenly sounding much nicer. "For somebody as pretty as you, I'll give you one freebie. Just be sure to tell all your friends about me, eh?"

"Oh, absolutely, I will!" said Monique, although none of her butterfly friends would have even thought of buying cotton candy from a spider. Unfortunately, hunger was making her forget things she should have remembered. Spud handed her a cone, which was twice as big as she was. "Can you hold it for me?" she asked.

"Of course, cutie! Here you go," he said with a frightening grin. Monique extended her proboscis and sucked the cotton candy down. It wasn't nectar but it was delicious, especially since she had hardly had anything to drink in two days. She coughed, and sipped some more, and this time some of it stuck to her mouth and nose. "Oooh! Kind of sticky," she said, trying to wipe it off with her wing. Unfortunately, her wing stuck to her mouth. Then she tried to use her left wing to free her right wing, and you guessed it: Now both wings were stuck to her face, making her look like the "speak no evil" monkey. "Oh, my goodness, this is embarrassing!" Monique said in a muffled voice. "Can you help me?"

"I'd be happy to," said Spud. But he had no intention of helping Monique. Instead, he twirled his hairy arms around her and dragged her behind the booth before she could even scream. He then reached one arm out, flipped the "Open" sign to "Closed" and disappeared behind the booth with his catch.

Chapter Seven

About this time, Charley's head popped out of a hole on the other side of the Carny Town wall. He spat dirt out of his mouth and looked around. "Okay, where is she?" he wondered aloud. But as Charley began to pass by the flashy booths and smell the amazing smells, he almost forgot about Monique. He had never seen anything like the colors, for one thing. In "Wormland," only Queen Martha was allowed to wear bright colors. But in Carny Town, gorgeous color was everywhere: lavender, indigo, turquoise, green, ocean blue, scarlet, yellow and orange. Suddenly Charley began to quiver. He looked down at himself and could see that once again, he was about to shed. "Uh-oh," he said, and darted behind the nearest booth. A minute later, a new Charley emerged, brighter and shinier than ever before. But this time, he wasn't ashamed. In fact, he actually strutted a little as he proceeded down the carnival's main pathway.

When he came to the Shooting Gallery, he stopped. An old grasshopper was shooting at the wooden birds. "Dang!" said the grasshopper as his gun went off, missing his mark. He fired again and again, missing every time.

The grasshopper looked suspiciously at Mike, the booth manager. "You've got it rigged, don't ya?"

"With shots as bad as you, grandpa, I don't have to!" said Mike. "Next!"

The grasshopper walked off, and Charley stepped up. He picked up the gun and fired, nailing a bird on the first try.

"Hey! You didn't pay!" said Mike.

"How much?" asked Charley.

"Five cents, kid!"

"Uh—my mom's over there," said Charley, untruthfully. He was pointing at a ladybug standing over by the stuffed bug booth. Mike squinted at them.

"That ain't yer mom," he said.

"Yes, it is," Charley lied. "I take after my dad."

"Yeah, yeah. Whatever—I'll give you one round, that's it!"

So Charley began to shoot, quickly zapping three more birds in a row. "So, what's my prize?" he asked.

"A chocolate covered cherry, or another round," said Mike. "Prizes get bigger the more times you win." "Awesome! I'll take one more round," said Charley. The wooden birds came flying out, and again he picked them off, *Pow! Pow! Pow!* Mike grudgingly took a small stuffed mouse from the prize bin and handed it to Charley.

"Thanks," he said. "But I'm going for *that* one." Charlie nodded at a huge teddy bear with a red bow around its neck, and again took aim.

Back at the Compost Café, White and Field were still living it up. Two of the dancing girls had joined them and were sitting on their laps.

"Did you really, Rocco? Did you really say that to that ugly old moth-queen?" one of them asked Field.

"I sure did," he said. "I said, "Lady, if you got any uglier I'd burst into tears! And sure enough—she got uglier, and I cried my eyes out!" At this the dancing girls laughed hysterically.

"Having a good time, officers?" wheezed an unpleasant voice behind them. White and Field whirled around to see Edgar and his horseflies, who had been quietly listening for some time now. Their jaws fell open and they sprang to attention, dumping the dancing girls off their laps.

"Your Highness, sir!" said White.

"Your Holiness, sir!" said Field.

"What a surprise to find you here in Carny Town," said Edgar in a sugary tone. "Decide to take a little time off for R & R, did we?"

"Y-y-yes, sir," said White, "We just thought we'd take a quick break, just a few minutes, before gettin' back to our search for the creature and the kid! We were just paying the check!"

"Yeah," Field piped up, "I kept tellin' him we'd better beat it, but—"

"SILENCE!" screamed Edgar at a deafening volume. "You dirty, despicable, rotten, lazy, unworthy, untrustworthy vermin! Get out of my sight, before my horseflies yank your legs off one by one!"

"B-b-but, sir, I swear, we were just—"

"Be gone!" roared Edgar. "If I ever see you again it will be at your execution!" And White and Field fled in terror, all the way out of Carny Town.

Edgar grandly stepped up to their table and sat down. "A round of drinks for my men and me, wench!" said he to the waitress.

"Vench! Who you calling a *vench*?" said the waitress, and stormed off, followed by the dancing girls.

"Well! Who needs this low-class establishment? Come on, men, we'll take our money elsewhere!" said Edgar, flying off in a huff. A second later Spud, who had been hiding behind the stage, crept out and slapped up a cardboard sign: "THE INCREDIBLE WINGED CREATURE! NEXT SHOW IN 5 MINUTES." And just as quickly he slithered behind the curtain.

Meanwhile, Charley was still at the Shooting Gallery, and getting better all the time. The bug customers lined up behind him were losing their patience.

"Come on! Let somebody else have a chance," said one.

"Yeah, that's enough, kid!" said Mike. "You're done!"

"Where's my prize?" asked Charley.

"Your prize was 10 free rounds," Mike scowled. "Now get out of my face, little worm!"

"I'm not a worm—I'm a caterpillar!" Charley said boldly, and handed his gun to the bug behind him. Just then, Edgar and the horseflies flew overhead.

"Hey, Mom! Look! Up in the sky," yelled a young bug. The crowd, who had never seen a flying insect, scattered instantly, leaving Charley exposed.

Spotting him, Edgar stopped and hovered in the air. "Having *fun*, son? Get him, flies!"

The horseflies zeroed in on Charley and prepared to attack. Charley took off, zig-zagging through the crowd; luckily he was smart enough not to run in a straight line. (Of course, flies have compound eyes, so from their point of view it looked like a whole bunch of caterpillars were sprinting through the crowd.) With that advantage, Charlie managed to make it as far as the Haunted House. He darted past the ticket booth, which was attended by a snoozing centipede, and slipped inside. Seconds later, Edgar and his flies arrived and followed him.

The Haunted House was just what you'd expect: skeletons, cobwebs, creaky floorboards and funhouse mirrors. Edgar and the flies entered and sniffed around for Charley, who seemed to have disappeared. "Here, little worm," called Edgar. "I know you're in here! You're sick, and we're here to help you!" At that moment a bug skeleton reached all its arms out toward Edgar, with a chilling "BWA-HA-HA-HA!" Edgar screamed and jumped back. The horseflies stifled their laughter.

"Ha ha ha, it's all in fun! Of course I knew that," said Edgar, recovering. "He's got to be in here somewhere—hello!" Edgar had just spotted a wooden coffin in the corner. He hopped over to it when suddenly it flew open by itself and another skeleton popped out, *BOING*!

"AHHHH!" Edgar screamed again. "Confound it! Maybe he went out the back way," said Edgar. He slammed the back door loudly, pointed at a large cobweb hanging from the ceiling, and motioned for the horseflies to hide in the shadows. After a few seconds, Charley's head emerged cautiously from a trap door in the floor. Quickly deciding that he was alone, he made a run for the back door.

"Now!" said Edgar, and the horseflies pulled the cobweb down on Charley.

"Game over," Edgar cried gleefully.

"Let me go!" Charley demanded. "What do you want from me?"

"It's not just you we want," Edgar replied. "Where is the alien creature?"

"I don't know what you're talking about," Charley fibbed.

"Don't bother to lie, you worthless worm," said Edgar. "You're going to take us to her. Maybe the fresh air will refresh your memory!"

So the horseflies towed him, tangled up in the cobweb, out of the Haunted House. They flew over Carny Town, and again all the bugs below began pointing at them.

"Tell us where she is, boy, or else," Edgar commanded. But Charley kept his mouth shut. "Very well! Drop him," he commanded.

The flies did as instructed, and Charley fell to the ground. He groaned a little, but he wasn't badly hurt, because caterpillars are actually quite flexible. He'd landed right in front of the Compost Café, with its new sign: "THE INCREDIBLE WINGED CREATURE! NEXT SHOW IN 2 MINUTES!"

Edgar landed beside him. "Well, well, well!" he said, looking at the sign. "Winged creature, eh? What an uncanny coincidence!"

"Trust me, that can't be her," Charley said quickly. "Mon—the flying thing left me a long time ago. She said she had to get out of the cave before her flock migrated, and she couldn't wait."

"Liar!" said Edgar, approaching the ticket booth. "I want tickets to the next show! Now!" he shouted, pounding on the little window.

Spud, now wearing a top hat and tails, crawled over the booth with an unfriendly smile. "Ahhh!" cried Edgar, hopping backwards. (Moths and spiders are not exactly friends by nature.) The he gulped and said, "We want to see the winged creature."

"For you and your party, only a dollar," said Spud.

"A dollar! That's outrageous," Edgar complained. "I'll give you fifty cents."

"And I'll take it," Spud replied. "But you'll still owe me fifty cents."

"Scoundrel! Don't you know who I am?" Edgar whined, his words sounding much more dangerous than his voice.

"Um . . . an ugly little Death's-head moth? The kind I used to eat three at a time for breakfast?"

"How dare you! I am Prince Edgar of Wormland!"

At this Spud started laughing hysterically. "Prince Edgar of *Worm-Worm-Worm-Wormland!* Ha ha ha! Stop, you're killing me!" Finally Spud stopped laughing and turned a deadly eye on Edgar. "One dollar," he repeated. "Not a penny less!"

"Oh, all right!" said Edgar, and pulled out the money. Spud snapped it up and crawled up onto the stage in front of the curtain. Edgar and the flies took their seats, guarding Charley's cobweb in the middle of them. Spud cleared his throat and spoke into the microphone.

"Gentlemen, I give you—the Incredible Winged Creature!" With a flourish he opened the curtains to reveal a very sad-looking Monique. Her wings drooped pitifully and there was a chain around one of her feet.

"Spread your wings, creature!" Spud ordered. "Sing!"

Monique slowly spread her wings, her head bowed with embarrassment. Her throat was parched and so dry that she could barely talk.

"I . . . can't."

"Yes, you can! Sing!" Spud commanded.

Charley was horrified, but kept quiet out of fear that he might make things worse for Monique. Edgar flew to the edge of the stage, never taking his eyes off of her.

"You are even more beautiful than I imagined, my dear," he leered. "I am Prince Edgar of Wormland," he bowed.

"Prince? Are you related to that horrible "queen"—that Martha-Moth person?" asked Monique.

"She is my mother, and she is not—well, actually she *is* kind of horrible," Edgar admitted. "Marry me, and I will make *you* queen!"

Charley couldn't keep still any longer. "She's not about to marry you, so you can forget about that!"

"Charley?" Monique whispered, squinting at her cobweb-covered friend. "Thank goodness! Look, mister . . . prince," she said to Edgar, trying to be nice. "Why don't you let my friend go? He hasn't done anything wrong."

"Unfortunately, I can't, my dear," said Edgar. "The child is contagious and must be quarantined immediately. If he is not treated, he could infect all of Wormland."

"It should be called 'Caterpillarland,' not 'Wormland,'" Monique said, trying not to sound angry. "And that's not true. He's not sick—he's changing into a butterfly, that's all. Now, let him go, please!"

"Again, my sweet, it's impossible," said Edgar, turning to Spud. "I would like to buy this creature from you. How much?"

"She's not for sale," said Spud.

"Everything's for sale," answered Edgar. "Name your price."

"I said she's not for sale," said Spud, pulling the curtain shut. "Now scram, Princey Poo! It's time for the next group."

Edgar shot Spud a haughty glare and flew past him, onto the stage. As he started to part the curtains, Spud licked his chops and opened his mouth wide. "Haven't had me a moth in ages," he purred. But before he could pounce, the horseflies flew to Edgar's rescue. For a few moments, dust and insect hair flew everywhere, and Charley couldn't tell who was winning. Seeing his opportunity, he threw off his cobweb. He clambered onto the stage and crawled under the curtain. Monique was struggling with the chain around her foot.

"Are you okay?" he asked her.

"Yes, but help me get this thing off!" she said. Charley yanked on the chain with all his hands and feet until it broke. They tiptoed offstage just as Edgar and Spud came up for air.

"They're getting away!" said Edgar.

"Run, Charley! Run! That way!" said Monique, knowing there was no way she could carry Charley in her weakened state. With a great effort she flapped her wings and flew toward Carny Town's western wall, toward the mouth of the cave. Charley ran, or crawled, that way too, but it was hopeless. The horseflies could still fly, and they were after him.

"Get that worm!" Edgar shouted, still in Spud's clutches.

"And bring back that butterfly, or your boss is going to be my lunch!" growled the spider, looking like he would make good on his promise.

The horseflies caught up to Charley in seconds and threw the cobweb back over him. Looking over her shoulder, Monique saw her friend being captured and froze. She hovered for a moment, torn with indecision. Finally she whispered, "I'm sorry!" And she flew over the wall.

"The creature is escaping," cried one of the horseflies, and took off after her. But at that moment an ear-splitting shriek sliced the air. The carnival customers, who recognized the sound, began to scatter before they even looked up. "BAT!" one of them screamed. "Run!"

What followed was complete chaos. Insects dug holes, threw their little ones in first, and dived in after them. The horseflies dropped Charley's cobweb and flew off in different directions, leaving Edgar to fend for himself. The bat, with its terrifying wingspan, loomed overhead like a death star. Charley covered his eyes and prepared for the worst, but the bat flew right past him. It was after Spud! The spider let go of Edgar and ran for his life. Edgar flattened his wings, camouflaging himself. Easily catching up to Spud, the bat swallowed him with a satisfied *gulp*. Then it flew away, probably in search of something more substantial for supper.

One by one, bugs poked their heads out of their hiding places. Charley, who was still tangled in his web, stumbled toward the Carny Town exit, tripping every few inches. Edgar, still traumatized by his near brush with death, saw the caterpillar hobbling away. "Oh, no, you don't!" he said, and flew after him. "I'm not going home empty-handed!" Edgar swooped Charley's cobweb up in his mouth and flapped his wings toward home, looking like a tiny stork carrying a knapsack. Charley squinted at the mouth of the cave. "Fly, Monique! Fly!" he whispered.

Chapter Eight

Monique was now flying as fast as she could towards the cave's mouth. But another day was almost over and it was getting dark, which meant it was also getting colder. She was weak from hunger, and as her body temperature dropped, she flew lower and more slowly. Her mouth was now so dry that she could barely remember what nectar tasted like. She knew she'd have to rest soon, but she was afraid that if she went to sleep, she might never wake up.

Then she heard a howling screech that echoed in the distance. "No, no," she said to herself. "Keep going—I'm almost there." She flapped her wings harder, but it didn't help. She simply couldn't fly any faster than she was already flying. She knew that she couldn't escape a bat by out-flying it, so she hovered and searched desperately for a place to hide. But it was too late. The bat was upon her, his mouth gaping, his wingspan terrifyingly wide. Monique jerked to her left as he swiped at her, catching the edge of her wing with his. "Ahhh!" Monique cried out in pain, then floated slowly to the ground.

The bat homed in on its dainty prey, now lying motionless on the cave's floor. But a split second before it could devour her, *WHOOSH!* The talons of a large owl swooped down and grabbed him. The bat shrieked and the owl hooted, carrying him off. Monique lay perfectly still, her wing badly torn, her face as pale as a ghost's. Then with another loud *HOOT*, the owl returned. He landed beside Monique and gently blew on her face until she opened one eye.

"Am I dead?" she asked.

"Not at all, my dear, *hoo hoo, hoo hoo*. My name is Herbert, I am pleased to meet you."

"You saved my life," said Monique gratefully.

"You had a close call, it's true, it's true. Come with me, I will mend your wing for you!"

"Oh, thank you so much, but I have to get out of here right away. My family is migrating, and—ow!" said Monique, gasping in pain as she tried to get up. "My wing!"

"You won't go far like that, *hoo hoo*. I will make it as good as new."

"No offense," Monique responded, "but I never heard of an owl who could fix a torn wing."

"Really, I can, it's true, it's true. Climb on my back if you would, *hoo hoo*."

So Monique climbed on Herbert's back, since she was completely out of options and had no choice but to trust him. She held on tight as Herbert flew through the cave, and in minutes they had arrived at his nest, which he had built into a hole in the cave's wall. It was clean as a whistle and by Monique's standards, enormous.

"Very nice place you have here," she said weakly as Herbert landed.

"Thank you, my dear, *hoo hoo, hoo hoo*. Be careful now, do do, do do." Monique slowly got off Herbert's back and flopped onto the floor of the nest.

"Ow! It hurts," she said, her torn wing dangling at her side.

"Stay where you are, *hoo hoo hoo hoo*. I have some nectar for you, I do."

"Really?" said Monique. It was almost too much to hope for. Herbert went to a small cupboard and came back with a jar clearly marked *Nectar*. He opened it and took out a spoonful for his guest. She dipped her proboscis in and took a long drink.   "Mmmm . . . that tastes heavenly!"

"You will have more, *hoo hoo hoo*," said Herbert. "But first I will mend your wing for you." Herbert went back to the cupboard and took out what looked like a small first-aid kit. Inside the kit was a jar marked *Wing Mender*. He dipped the tiniest bit of his own wing into it, then touched Monique's torn wing. As if by magic, the tear in the wing disappeared and it was perfect again.

"A healing concoction for you, *hoo hoo*!"

Monique couldn't believe her eyes. "Well, I thank you so much, really, I do!" Monique blinked twice, realizing that she had accidentally rhymed her sentence with Herbert's.

"Think nothing of it, my dear, *hoo hoo*. Now, what else can I do for you?"

"Nothing that I can think of, sir," said Monique. "You've been so kind. Can you just show me the way out? Everything is such a blur."

"Only too happy to, *hoo hoo*," said Herbert. "Your family must be missing you."

"Yes," she said. She flapped her wings to test them, flew to the door of the nest, and hesitated. "Herbert . . . I have a question for you."

"Of course, of course, hoo hoo, hoo hoo."

"Well—it's about my friend Charley, the caterpillar. He got caught, and I got away. I feel like I should go back."

"That would be difficult, *hoo hoo, hoo hoo*. Are you sure that is what you want to do?"

"I don't know," said Monique. "I'm dying to get home, but I can't stand to think about what might happen to him. Do you know about the moth-queen, Queen Martha?"

"Yes, my dear, I do, I do," said Herbert ruefully. "She calls herself a queen, but it isn't true."

"Then why do the caterpillars obey her? Why don't they just run away?""It's hard to understand, *hoo hoo, hoo hoo*. I'll tell you the truth if you want me to."

And with the Outside World just a short flight away, Monique sat down. "I do," she said. "Please, do."

Edgar had by this time almost reached the castle, surprising even himself at how fast he could fly with Charley's web in his mouth. The truth was, he was so frightened about another bat attack that it gave him plenty of motivation. As soon as he was inside the castle he spat, dumping Charley on the floor.

"Yecch!" he said. "Is there anything worse than flying three miles with a sick worm in your mouth? Guards!" Ten or twelve cockroaches goose-stepped out of the woodwork to greet him.

"Guard the worm while I advise the queen of what's happened," he continued. "When I call for you, bring him in."

"Yes, sir!"

Now, Edgar knew that his mother would be extremely angry when she found out that he had returned with no Monique and no butterfly wings, and he dreaded telling her. Summoning all his courage, he entered her chambers and saw her sitting in front of her vanity.

"It isn't fair! It isn't fair," the old moth mumbled to her unattractive reflection.

"Hello, Mother! I'm home!" Edgar chortled cheerfully. Martha spun around and saw that Edgar was empty-handed.

"Well? Where are the wings?"

"Well, you see," Edgar began as he hopped into the room. "She, um, well, it's unfortunate but I think you'll be happy with what I was able to accomplish."

"I'm waiting!" said the queen.

"Guards!" croaked Edgar. "Present the prisoner!" Two of the guards entered carrying Charley's cobweb, which was now attached to a long stick balanced on their shoulders. "Ta-da!" said Edgar. "Congratulations, you captured a sick worm," said Martha, her tone sarcastic. "Where is the alien creature?"

The truth is, Mother, I almost had her. In fact I absolutely, most certainly *did* have her, but I was attacked by an army of giant bats and all the horseflies deserted me. I am lucky to have escaped with my life! Unfortunately, the creature perished. Torn to bits, actually. Nothing left."

"That's a lie!" Charlie burst out. "She's not dead. She got away!"

"Silence, worm!" said Edgar.

Martha, shocked at Charley's spunk, almost spit out something nasty at him. But changing her mind, her face softened.

"On the contrary. Tell me what happened . . . *Charley*," she purred, in the sweetest voice she could muster.

"Let me out of this thing, and I will," said Charley.

"No!" screamed Edgar.

"Let him out, guards," Martha said coolly. The guards glanced at each other, then set about freeing Charley from his cobweb. Soon he was standing in front of the queen, looking surprisingly calm. "Well? Speak!" Martha commanded.

"Okay, first of all, she's not an 'alien creature.' She's a butterfly, and her name's Monique," said Charley.

"Ah, I see! And where is 'Monique' now?" asked Martha, as sweet as sugar.

"I don't know, but she's not dead. She got away. At least—I hope she did, because she saved my life."

"That remains to be seen, worm!" said Edgar.

The old moth turned on her son. "Edgar, you break my heart. You lied to me."

"No! I—well, you see, everything happened so fast. Monster bats everywhere, killing everything in sight. Even if they didn't get her at that moment, I'm sure they've gotten her by now."

"But you don't know that to be a fact," said Martha. "Do you?"

"Well, not exactly. But as I said—"

"DON'T EVER LIE TO ME AGAIN, BOY!" screamed Martha.

"Yes, Mother," the red-faced Edgar answered.

"Take this worm to the infirmary," said Martha, addressing the guards. "You know what to do with him there."

"Come on, kid. March!" said the guard.

"I—I can't," said Charley, looking at his feet. It was true. Charley's chrysalis had begun encircling his feet and was rapidly climbing up his body.

"How dare you *change* in front of me!" hissed the queen.

"I can't help it," said Charley. "I'm—I'm going to be a butterfly!" Charley looked around instinctively, did a back flip, and attached himself to the top of the doorframe. As he hung upside down, the chrysalis slid closer and closer to his head.

"Oh, I don't think so," said Martha evenly. "As soon as your shell has hardened, it will be cracked, and your silk threads put to good use!"

"Why?" asked Charley. "You can't really be that mean!"

"On the contrary, I'm not mean, I'm practical," said Martha. "What good is a worm that can't work?"

"Please—tell my mom that I love her. My dad, too," said Charley, just before the chrysalis enveloped his face. Charley the caterpillar had disappeared, and a bright green cocoon hung in his place. For a moment everyone stared at it, speechless. Finally, Martha spoke.

"I've just had a delicious idea," she smiled. "Take the thing to the public square," she continued. "Hang it there and leave it for a few days. It will serve as a warning to any worms who are tempted to change in the future. Then we'll simply take it down and bury it before it hatches. That should take care of any threat of rebellion."

"Brilliant, Mother! Brilliant!" said Edgar, flapping his wings dramatically. "Perhaps tomorrow I can again go in search of the creature!"

"I think not, Edgar," said the queen, her jaw clenched. "You will *never* leave this castle again, do you hear? Now, go to your room!"

Edgar's face blushed a deep purple at this humiliating treatment. After he was gone, they removed Charley's chrysalis from the door, bowed to the queen and marched out, carrying it horizontally like a coffin.

Martha rolled her wheel chair over to her dresser drawer and opened it. She took out a stack of pictures of beautiful butterflies and looked through them until she came to one of an orange-and-black monarch.

"So, you have escaped me this time," she said. "But my next pair of wings will be even more beautiful than yours." Then she began to laugh—a very ugly laugh, indeed.

Fred looked at the factory clock: It was ten minutes to five. As usual, Cathy was barely turning her spinning wheel.

"We're almost done, sweetie!" he said. "What's for dinner tonight?"

Cathy shot him a look but said nothing. Suddenly static crackled over the loudspeaker and Edgar appeared on the TV screen.

"Attention, worms! You are all ordered to report to the public square immediately. I repeat, immediately!"

"What now?" asked Cathy.

"I don't know," said Fred, "but it can't be good."

"You heard the prince! Everybody out!" yelled the guard.

As the caterpillar workers exited the factory, the off-duty caterpillars emerged from their homes. When they had all gathered in the public square, the doors of the queen's chamber flew open and Edgar pushed Martha out onto the balcony in her wheelchair. Her fake wings flapped mechanically as she spoke into a microphone.

"Citizens of Wormland!" she croaked. "We have good news and bad news to report today. On the bright side, the kidnapped worm has been found!"

"Charley?" Cathy cried out. Fred immediately put his hand over her mouth.

"Unfortunately, by the time he was captured, his illness was irreversible," the queen went on. "There is nothing now that can be done for him. But every cloud has a silver lining! We have decided to put him on display as a warning, so that this tragedy does not happen again. Bring him out, guards!"

The castle's drawbridge lowered and two guards marched out in single file, carrying a pole from which Charley's chrysalis dangled. The crowd parted as the cockroaches carried it onto a platform in the middle of the square and stood at attention. The caterpillars all gasped in unison.

"Behold, the fate of the worm with changing fever!" declared Martha.

Cathy furiously pushed her way through the crowd to the front of the rope line. "That's my son! That's my son!"

No one made a move. "Come on, honey, let's go home," said Fred. Ignoring him, Cathy jumped over the rope and in an instant was on the platform. She ran toward the chrysalis and put her arms around it.

"My baby! My baby!" she sobbed. The guards yanked her away and roughly escorted her down the platform steps, pushing her in Fred's direction. Claire, who had been standing nearby, came over and shyly put an arm around her friend's mom.

"It's okay, Mrs. Littlefield. I'm sure that's not Charley," she whispered. "They probably just rigged something up to scare everybody."

"That's right, Cath," said Fred, but Cathy continued to cry.

At that moment Edgar flew out of the castle and hovered above the platform. He cleared his throat dramatically. "Now hear this, worms!" he began. "The sick child was not given emergency treatment and as a result of his escape attempt, has died. The queen has generously decided to leave his remains here for public viewing as a reminder of what happens to all worms who change. After a few days' time, he will be given a proper burial. That is all! You are dismissed. Back to your huts, or to work, or wherever you're supposed to be!" With that he turned and flew back to Martha's balcony, where they both waved grandly to the crowd, and went inside.

One by one, the caterpillars began to disperse until only Cathy, Fred and Claire were left, staring up at the platform and the lonely chrysalis that hung there.

By this time Herbert was in the middle of telling Monique the story of how Martha had become "queen." It took him a long time to tell it, because of course he ended every sentence with "hoo hoo, hoo hoo." In fact, he didn't finish until almost dawn. This is how it went:

As a young moth, Martha had believed she was ugly. She was jealous of anything she felt was more attractive than she was, especially butterflies. One day, as Martha was watching several butterflies sip from their favorite flowers, she noticed a young Painted Lady butterfly who made her especially jealous. (She stood out because her wings were a bit brighter than all the others.) When the butterfly noticed Martha staring at her, the moth's eyes literally green with envy, she instinctively flew away. Martha followed her, and the Painted Lady kept flying until she came to a big hole in the side of a hill—the mouth of a cave. She flew in and hid, thinking that she had escaped the moth.

The young butterfly had mated, and was ready to lay eggs. She found a safe-looking spot to rest, and soon a small mountain of eggs was lying underneath her. "Be safe, my darlings!" she said, and flew back out of the cave.

As soon as she was gone, Martha peeked out from where she had been hiding. Seeing the eggs, she felt another pang of jealousy. Suddenly Martha herself began to lay! She huffed and puffed, but try as she might, only one tiny egg appeared. Compared to the pile of eggs the lovely butterfly had just laid, it was rather pitiful.

Just then, the whole cave began to shake. But before Martha could escape, the earthquake had almost completely sealed the mouth of the cave with mud and rocks. And for the first time in her life, Martha herself was afraid. She turned around and surveyed the pile of butterfly eggs the young monarch had left, and laughed wickedly. "I guess you're mine now, *darlings*!" It was then that Martha had what she thought was her first brilliant idea: she would pretend to be the eggs' mother when they turned into caterpillars. She would tell them they were silkworms and teach them to spin the silk that she imagined would make her beautiful. If they were never allowed to turn into butterflies, Martha would always be the most beautiful creature in the cave, and certainly the only one who could fly. She made use of her naturally forceful personality, enlisting cockroaches and horseflies to work for her. Although she had no real power, she made them *believe* that she did by speaking in a fierce and unkind way. Eventually the horseflies began going on regular caterpillar-hunting expeditions in the Outside World. They would simply trap them, kidnap them, and bring them back to their mad queen.

After Herbert had finished his story, Monique was silent for a moment. "You mean that the only reason the caterpillars don't change is because they *think* they can't?" she asked.

"Whatever you think you can do, you do. But the opposite also is true, *hoo hoo!*"

Monique whistled. "Wow, that's crazy! But the anti-change medication—where did she get that?"

"Nothing but birdseed, *hoo hoo, hoo hoo*," said Herbert.

"Unbelievable!" sighed Monique, with a shake of her head. "Can't *you* help them somehow, Herbert?"

"My dear, I would like to, *hoo, hoo, hoo*. I could tell them it's all been a ruse, it's true. But they wouldn't believe an old owl, *hoo hoo*. It is up to them to choose what to do."

"I see," said Monique, looking very uncomfortable. "Well—I really must be going. What do you think will happen to Charley?"

"There's probably nothing that you can do," said the owl. "Try not to worry, my dear, *hoo hoo*."

"Yes, you're right . . . who ever heard of a worried butterfly? That would be silly!" But Monique *was* worried, and it showed.

The owl then escorted Monique to the mouth of the cave, where she hugged him (or as much of him as she could hug), said goodbye, and flew out of the cave into the brilliant morning sunshine.

Chapter Nine

Finally free, Monique was immediately struck by how beautiful and colorful everything was in the Outside World. It was much more vivid than she remembered.

"Hey, everybody! I'm back!" she yelled.

There was no answer. A few birds flew by, twittering. Monique looked around and realized that she was probably a long way from the part of the forest where she had originally fallen into the cave. Why had she expected the flock to be here waiting for her? Suddenly she felt lonelier than she had in her whole life.

She sighed. Noticing a bunch of inviting-looking pansies, she flew over to them and took a long drink. "Not bad," she said. Spotting some purple phlox nearby, she sipped from them as well. "Why don't they taste good?" she asked herself.

Monique flew to a large maple tree branch and perched on it. Looking up, she saw a chrysalis hanging from a branch above her. She gasped; for some reason, it almost looked scary. Then she remembered her promise to Charley at the entrance to Carny Town.

"Don't leave the cave without me, okay?" Charley had begged. And Monique had promised him that she wouldn't.

"I couldn't help it. I had to," she said aloud, although there was no one there to hear her. Where was Tiger? She couldn't believe he would have left her. "TIGER!" she yelled at the top of her lungs. "TIIIIIIII-GERRRRRR!"

At that moment, Tiger was flying around in circles, looking for Monique. The rest of the flock had headed to Mexico the day before, having given up the search for her. "I should never have left her alone," he muttered. "It's all my fault!" Just then Tiger heard a voice in the distance—a very familiar voice. He listened, then heard it again.

"TIIIIIIII-GERRRRRR!"

Tiger spun around, looking in all directions. "Monique? MONIQUE! I'm over here!"

Monique and Tiger kept shouting each other's names, flying closer and closer to each other. Finally Monique saw a speck of yellow, and Tiger saw a speck of orange and blue. Within seconds they were together, hugging.

"Where the heck have you been?" Tiger asked her. "I've been looking all over for you! We thought for sure the humans had . . . ."

"I know," said Monique. "I'm so sorry. They were chasing me and I tried to hide, but I accidentally ended up in this cave where—oh, Tiger, I thought I'd never see you again!"

"Well, you're back now, and I'm not letting you out of my sight!" said Tiger. "Come on. The others have gone, but if we hurry, we might be able to catch up with them."

Tiger turned and started to fly away, but Monique hovered in the air. "Wait!" she said. "I've got to think!"

"What do you mean? We've got to get to Mexico. We're three days late!"

"Okay, look," said Monique, zipping over to a tree branch. "This is going to sound crazy, but you've got to believe me. In that cave—in there—are hundreds of caterpillars who don't change . . . just because they've been brainwashed to think they're worms. They don't know about the real world, or caterpillars, or butterflies, or anything!" This wicked moth-queen even named the place "Wormland." They have to work for her, spinning silk every day, because she can't get enough of the stuff. It's horrible!" Monique covered her face with her wings.

"That's awful," said Tiger, who really thought Monique must have had a very bad dream. "Sweetie, you're tired. We've got to get you some nectar, pronto! Look—over there!"

"I don't want any nectar," said Monique.

Tiger, who was already halfway to a bunch of tulips, turned in mid-flight and stared at her. "What did you say?"

"My friend is in trouble. He's changing, and the queen's probably going to kill him."

"He? Who's he?" asked Tiger, suddenly a little jealous.

"He's a kid, just a caterpillar. They've captured him, and—oh, it's complicated, but the thing is—he *needs* me," said Monique.

"Well, I need you, too," answered Tiger. "Now, come on, let's go!"

"I can't," said Monique.

She had made her decision. Turning around, she flew back toward the cave's mouth. Tiger couldn't believe his eyes.

"Monique! You've *got* to come with me! If you fly back in that cave, I can't wait for you any longer!"

Monique stopped in mid-air and looked at him. "I'll miss you. I love you!" And she was gone.

Back at the factory, Cathy was at her spinning wheel, staring zombie-like into space. Betty, the caterpillar to her left, noticed her expression. "Cathy," she began, "I've been wanting to tell you . . . I'm so sorry about what happened to your son. It's just terrible."

"Yeah, thanks," said Cathy. "You'll never understand it unless it happens to you."

Just then the loudspeaker crackled and Edgar's voice blared: "Attention, workers! It has come to the queen's attention that silk production has decreased drastically in the last few weeks. Therefore, you will all be required to work two hours of overtime each day, beginning immediately and until further notice. That is all. Carry on!"

The caterpillars grumbled under their breath. "Two hours? With no extra pay?" said one.

"What, you want more work and extra pay, too?" muttered another one.

Cathy slowed down on her wheel until she came to a full stop.

"I won't do it any more," she announced. Fred and all the other caterpillars turned and looked at her.

"*What did you say, worm?*" snarled the factory boss.

"I have a name—it's Cathy!" she answered. "And I said I won't do it any more."

"All right, then, *Cathy*," said the boss mockingly. "Get back to work, or you're under arrest!"

"Do what you gotta do, officer," said Cathy, folding all of six of her arms across her chest. The guard turned purple with anger. He blew his whistle, and two more cockroach guards ran in. "That one back there," he said, pointing at Cathy.

But as they marched back toward Cathy and prepared to handcuff her, they noticed that something strange was happening. Cathy was quivering all over. She was changing!

"Are you okay? What's the matter?" Fred asked his wife nervously.

And before you could say "metamorphosis," Cathy had shed her skin. She picked up the old skin and looked at it. "Woo!" she said. "That was interesting!"

The factory boss exploded. "You are under arrest in the name of the queen! You have no right to remain silent, no right to talk, no right to an attorney . . . basically no rights at all!"

Cathy held her head high as the boss handcuffed her and led her out of the factory. For a second there was silence, then Fred spoke up.

"If they take her, they've got to take me!" he said.

"Yeah, the same goes for me!" said Betty.

"And me!" another caterpillar chimed in.

"And me, too!"

"Come on, guys!" said Fred, and headed to the door. One by one the other caterpillars followed him, calm but determined. As they walked out, the cockroach guard stationed outside jumped up and down and blew his whistle, but the caterpillars kept marching. They followed the factory boss, who led Cathy past the platform where Charley's chrysalis hung. He intended to take her to the castle and deliver her to Queen Martha. But suddenly she stopped in her tracks. "I'm not going to go a step farther! Not until you take my son down from there!" she cried. Fred and the other caterpillars quickly caught up to them.

"Yeah! Take him down! Take him down!" they yelled.

The factory boss blew his whistle three times. Dozens more cockroach guards instantly emerged from all directions, encircling the caterpillars with a long rope. "Squeeze 'em!" they hollered. Then the caterpillars did something they'd never done before: they fought back. The caterpillars outnumbered the cockroach guards, and a wild and woolly free-for-all broke out. Fred took a swing at a guard, who punched him back, sending him reeling. Landing in front of Charley's platform, Fred looked up. What he saw made him gasp. "Look!" he cried.

Monique had returned and was hovering right above Charley's chrysalis. "LET—THEM—GO!" she hollered, in the toughest voice she could muster. The shocked guards dropped the rope.

"B-b-b-but only the queen and her son can fly," stammered one of the guards.

"Oh yeah?" said Monique. She made a few fancy circle 8's, proving them wrong.

"Alien creature! Alien creature!" the cockroaches screamed, running around like so many headless chickens. Monique alighted on the platform and the crowd gasped, unsure whether to be afraid or awestruck.

Still in handcuffs, Cathy wrestled away from the guards and addressed Monique. "You! This is all your fault! You're the one who took my boy."

"I'm sorry, ma'am," said Monique. "I was just trying to help."

"Well, you didn't!" said Cathy. "He's dead!"

Monique glanced at the chrysalis. "Dead! He's not dead. He's about to become a butterfly, like me!"

"Ha! What do you think we are, stupid?" asked Fred.

And the other caterpillars joined in with shouts of "Yeah, we're not dumb!" "Give us a break!" "That's a lie!" "We're sick of being lied to!" And so forth.

Hearing the commotion, Martha hobbled to the window. When she saw Monique, she clutched at her throat. "B-B-B-B-butter—" she began.

"What is it, Mother? Spit it out," Edgar yawned from his perch.

"The butterfly! She's back!" Martha choked.

Edgar turned a page in the book he was reading without even looking up. "You're paranoid, Mother. You're having a delusion."

Martha took off her crown and flung it at Edgar, connecting squarely with his head. "*GET ME THOSE WINGS!*" she screamed.

Edgar hopped over to the window. Seeing Monique, his eyes once again almost popped out of his head. He flew out the window and over the crowd, landing in front of Monique on the platform.

"Hello, my dear! What a pleasant surprise," he said in a nasal whine. "Unfortunately, you've put me in a bit of an awkward spot. I'm going to have to ask you for your wings."

"They don't come off," said Monique.

"Then we'll have to find a way to *get* them off. Guards!"

Two of the cockroach guards twirled their ropes, lassoing Monique's torso. The caterpillars fell back. Then, there was a loud *crack*! Charley's chrysalis was breaking open.

"Yes, Charley! Push! Push!" cried Monique, ignoring the ropes around her waist.

The cocoon splintered a few more times, then hatched open like an egg. A dripping, blue butterfly emerged. He shook off his wings, splattering thick goo everywhere. "Look at me," said Charley. "I'm a butterfly!"

Cathy rushed onto the platform. "Charley? Is that really you?"

"What did I tell you?" said Monique. "Not that I'm one to say I told you so."

Charley spread his wet wings. "Yes, Mom, it's me! Check it out!" He did a little test flight and immediately fell back on the platform. He tried again, and this time stayed in the air. Edgar, the guards and the caterpillars all gawked in amazement as Charley soared above their heads.

Suddenly a high-pitched scream erupted from the balcony. It was Martha. "*GET ME THOSE WINGS!*" she howled.

Edgar threw back his chest, trying to look as important as possible. "All right, guards! On the count of three!" A guard on each side of Monique grabbed one of her wings and prepared to pull. "ONE—TWO—"

"No!" Charley screamed.

At that moment, everyone heard a whirring noise that sounded like a thousand tiny airplanes. All the insects turned around and looked in the direction it was coming from. Hundreds of monarchs, looking like a fleet of World War I flying aces, were approaching! Tiger and Marcus led the flock. Swooping down to the platform, Tiger hovered in front of the shocked guards, who still had Monique in their clutches. "Get your nasty hands off her!" he shouted.

The terrified Edgar almost choked, then found his voice. "Ahem! Who are you to give orders in my kingdom?" he said, his voice cracking. "This creature kidnapped one of our—"

But before Edgar could finish his sentence, Tiger boxed him in the face with his antennae, knocking him out cold. The monarchs then went after the cockroach guards, but seeing that they were outnumbered, the cockroaches simply slithered off into the cave.

Tiger darted over to Monique and helped her out of her ropes. "How in the world did you get them to come with you?" she asked him, referring to the monarch flock.

"Your dad had something to do with it," said Tiger. Marcus flew over to them.

"Daddy!" said Monique, hugging him.

"Hello, sweet pea," said Marcus. "When Tiger told me you had gone back to help your friend, I knew we had to do something to help, too."

Monique nodded and addressed the crowd. "Listen to me, my friends! You were never worms, but caterpillars, destined to be butterflies. Your 'queen' is just a crippled old moth who's brainwashed you into forgetting who you are! You are meant to fly, like all of us! Come with us to the Outside World, where changing is not only allowed, but encouraged. Pick a ride, everybody . . . we're out of here!"

And one by one, each caterpillar chose a butterfly.

Martha looked on from the balcony in horror. "*GUARDS! GUARDS! ATTACK! ATTACK!*" Curious for a look at the moth-queen, Monique flew up to the balcony and alighted on the ledge.

"*You're* the dreaded Queen Martha? Why, you can't even fly!" said Monique, seeing the moth's wheelchair.

"Of course I can fly! I'm just tired, that's all," protested Martha, unconvincingly.

"Well, you'll have plenty of time to rest up, now that there won't be anyone around for you to bully. I suggest you start taking power naps, and meditating. See ya, lady!"

Monique flew back down to Cathy and offered her back. "It would be my honor, Mrs. Littlefield," she said. Charley gave Claire a ride, and Tiger picked up Fred. And together, they all left "Wormland" for the last time, whooping for joy.

"Wait for me!" yelled Edgar, flapping his wings as fast as he could.

"Edgar! Where are you going?" croaked his mother.

"To get my own apartment!" he yelled back.

Martha continued to weep and wail as even her son deserted her. "Who will make my clothes? Who will I rule? Who will fear me?" *Fear me? Fear me?* Her voice echoed through the cave.

Rocco and Ricky, the former Lt. White and Sgt. Field, timidly stuck their heads out from behind a rock. "I don't know about you, but I'm with them," said White, referring to the butterflies.

"You'd better believe it," said Field. And the two cockroaches again headed toward the Outside World as fast as they could hop.

This time, the trip through the cave seemed to take no time at all. One of the first to emerge from the cave, Charley spotted a patch of milkweed and came in for a landing. Claire jumped off his back, delighted.

"Eat all you want!" he told her. "The fatter you get, the faster you'll be a butterfly!"

Monique and Tiger landed on a leafy tree branch and Cathy and Fred jumped off.

"My goodness!" said Cathy.

"Woohoo, free food!" said Fred.

At almost exactly the same moment, Tiger and Monique spotted a gorgeous butterfly bush covered with blossoms. They smiled at each other. "It's so good to have you back, kid," said Tiger. "Need a buddy?"

"I thought you'd never ask!" said Monique, and kissed him, right on the lips. Once again, Tiger saw stars.

"After you, beautiful," he said, pointing to a spectacular Pink Lady rose bush.

Monique floated down to it and took a long sip of nectar. "Ahhh!" she sighed. "Now, *that* is special."

THE END

ABOUT THE AUTHOR

Roxanne Beck is a freelance writer, actor, and singer. Originally from Arkansas, she holds a BA in English from Harding College and an MFA in screenwriting from UCLA's School of Theater, Film and Television. While at UCLA she was the recipient of the Oliver's Prize for the screenplay version of *Caterpillarland* and a Humanitas Drama Fellowship nominee for her sci-fi script *The Intenders*. *Caterpillarland* is her first book. Roxanne lives in Los Angeles with her wonderful dog Truman. More information is available at roxannebeck.com.

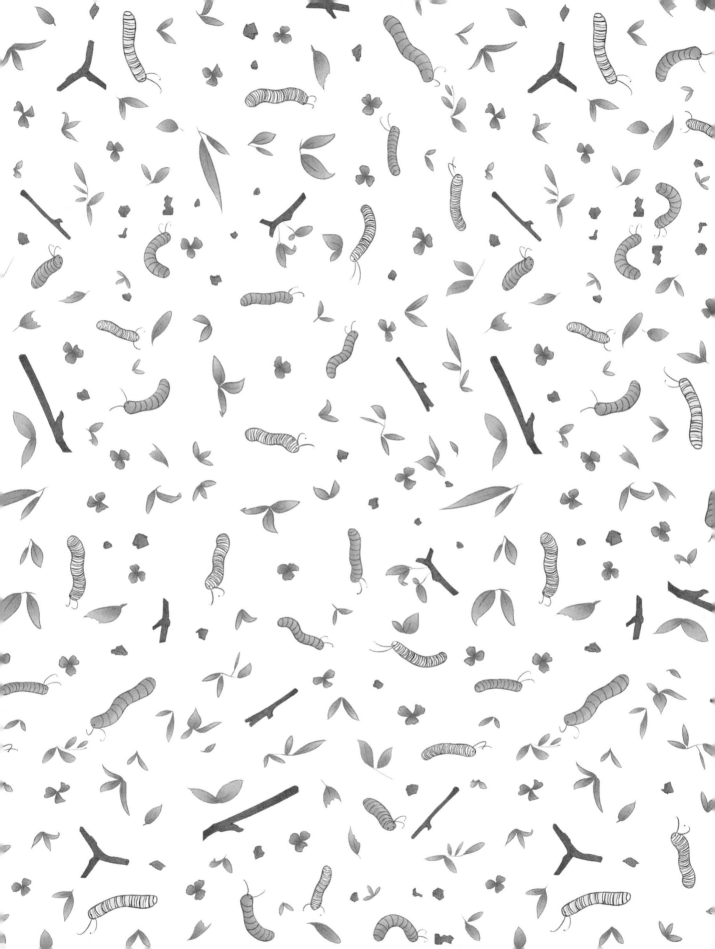

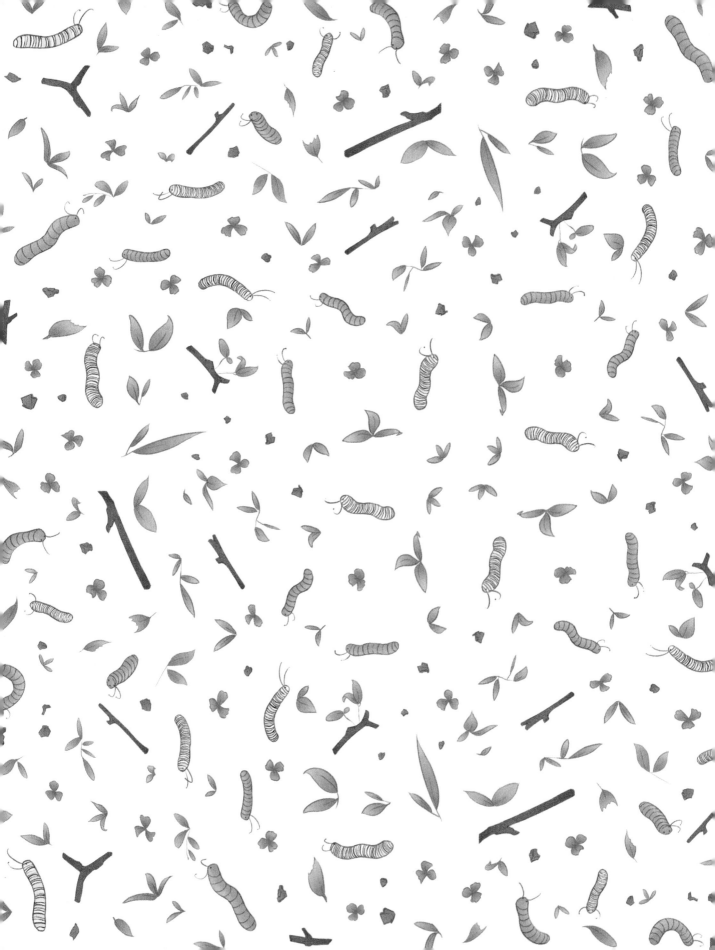

CPSIA information can be obtained at www.ICGtesting.com
Printed in the USA
BVOW07*0552230915

419293BV00012B/29/P